MW00366699

BOOK 1

TORY ANDREWS AND THE JUNIOR DEPUTIES

THE HOUSE OF TUNNELS

BOOK 1

TOBY ANDREWS AND THE JUNIOR DEPUTIES

THE
HOUSE OF TUNNELS

JERRY B. JENKINS
Author of The Dallas O'Neill Mystery Series

MOODY PRESS
CHICAGO

JL
J417h

© 1996 by
JERRY B. JENKINS

ISBN: 0-8024-1625-X

1 3 5 7 9 10 8 6 4 2

Printed in the United States of America

To Michael Bruce Jenkins,
who keeps me young

Contents

The Move

I admit it, I wanted to be a hero. I didn't know it would have anything to do with our new house. All I knew was that I had seemed to disappear for a couple of years, and now I wanted the world to know who I was. I dreamed of being on the news, of having my picture on the front page of the *Kalamazoo Gazette,* of everybody at church and school and in the neighborhood knowing who I was.

I guess that wasn't so unusual. Everybody wants to be somebody. Some people, like my mom and dad, would rather blend into the crowd. Not me or my friends. Being heroes sounded good to us. We just didn't know how to make it happen.

I already had plenty to be proud of. My dad was county deputy sheriff, one of the youngest to ever have that job. Lots of people asked me if it was hard having a dad who's a cop.

Dad didn't even like the word *cop.* He said it sounded disrespectful. So I always said, "My dad's not a cop. He's a law enforcement officer, a deputy with the sheriff's police."

But still, people wanted to know if it was embarrassing or if I couldn't be myself because my dad wore a badge and carried a gun. I didn't get it. Maybe some kids wouldn't want their dad to be a sheriff, but it made me proud.

People say the same thing about pastors' kids. At least that's what our pastor's son said. Only thing is, he agreed. He hated being a pastor's kid. Mom said he'd grow out of it and would probably be proud of his dad someday too.

"It wouldn't surprise me if he became a pastor himself," she said.

I couldn't imagine that, but Mom was usually right about that kind of stuff.

Anyway, I liked being a PK, which is something they call both preachers' kids and policemen's kids. Sometimes I pretended to know more than I really did about my dad's job, and when I was younger I even made up stories about dangerous cases to make Dad seem more important than ever. I figured that if he was important, I was important.

I learned the hard way not to exaggerate, which is just a nice word for lying. But I still wanted to be a hero, to save somebody's life or help my dad solve a case, or something. I'd felt that way for two years, ever since I was ten. Two years. That's how long I felt invisible.

I wasn't really invisible, of course. It's just that my little sister, Kate—she's eight now—and I sort of had to just stay out of the way while our older brother, Jason, was dying.

Of course, that's sure not the kind of attention I wanted. Jason was fourteen when he got cancer and sixteen when he died, and I knew he would have traded all his visitors and gifts and flowers and cards to be healthy again.

But there were times when I was jealous because it seemed as if he was the only kid in the family. Everything seemed to be centered on him. He got my bedroom, because it was on the first floor, and it was easier for Mom to get to when she took care of him. It was easier for all his visitors too.

Jason was the one who got asked about and prayed for at church. I loved him, and I felt guilty about sometimes holding it against him because all of a sudden it was as if Kate and I didn't exist.

We knew he was going to die; Dad had prepared us pretty well for that. We just didn't know when.

I argued with my dad. I told him I was praying hard and that I had a feeling God was going to heal Jason. I was mad that Dad didn't seem to have much faith. He said he did, but he also said we had to be realistic. The doctors didn't give Jason much hope, and as much as we hated it and wished it wasn't true, he would likely die soon.

When Jason did die, I guess it was better that Dad had prepared us, but it didn't seem to hurt any less. Kate still refused to sleep alone. She was afraid. I wasn't scared, but it sure was eerie, thinking Jason was still around when he wasn't.

I didn't cry at first, not even at the funeral. I knew people were worried about me, but I just couldn't cry. I was sad. Dad said I was stunned. That made the most sense to me. Some people sobbed. I just sat there. I couldn't talk. I couldn't smile or laugh. I didn't feel anything. Just stunned. Dad was right.

Then, about three days later, I started crying and couldn't stop. It wasn't that Jason was some perfect brother or anything. The three of us were all four years apart, and I know I bothered him. He bothered me sometimes too. But we got along pretty well, and I missed him something awful. It was like I got cheated out of having a high school brother, which is something any kid wants if he can't be the oldest himself.

The problem was, I don't think Mom or Dad understood how much it hurt Kate and me that Jason was gone. I felt left out and wanted some attention after two years of feeling in the way.

Getting attention wasn't all I thought it would be, though. There was bad with the good. None of what happened would have happened if we had stayed on the ranch after Jason died, so I was glad we moved. Dad wasn't glad, and neither was Kate, but there was really no choice.

I knew about the move before Kate did, but that was by accident. I was wide awake in the middle of the night, thinking about Jason. I tiptoed down the hall to see if Mom and Dad were awake, and I heard them talking. I shouldn't have stood there listening, but I was curious.

Dad was saying, "Hon, everybody we've talked to says moving is a mistake. You're not going to run from your grief. It'll be just as hard somewhere else. Jason will still be gone."

"I know," she said, beginning to cry, "but I just can't stand it here anymore. Everything reminds me of him. I can't do anything without thinking of him!"

They were quiet for a few moments. "I don't understand wanting to move into town, though, Lynn. Most people are moving *out* of the neighborhoods and into the country. This is what we've always wanted."

"I know. But we don't have Jason to help keep the place up, and—"

"Toby's getting bigger all the time. Have you noticed?"

She didn't say anything. I hoped she nodded. It wouldn't have surprised me if she hadn't noticed how tall I was at twelve. I was looking forward to doing the stuff Jason got to do before he got sick. He trimmed hedges, drove the riding mower, things like that. If we moved into town, I'd be pushing a mower like everybody else.

"I don't ask you for much, Phil," she said. "Do I?"

"Of course not."

"Well, now I'm begging you. I can't stand it here anymore. Tell me we can move."

"I can't talk you out of it?"

"You could forbid it. I know that. But please don't. I feel

like I'm drowning—like I'll never get over this. For my sanity, I have to get out of this place."

"That Victorian is for sale—the one you've always liked."

"Are you serious? The one in Oakwood?"

"Yup. Noticed it when I drove by the other day."

I didn't even know what a Victorian was, but I knew that house. Mom said something about it every time we passed it.

"Can I go see it tomorrow?"

"If you really want to."

"You'll never know how much I want to."

They started talking about what they could afford and all that. Dad said something about its being out of our price range except for how much our ranch was worth by now. By the time I went back to bed, I knew Mom would be looking at that Victorian and that we could probably afford it.

I would miss the ranch. I was a baby when we had moved out there, so I didn't know what it was like to live with neighbors right next door. For years Mom and Dad had said they never wanted to live in a neighborhood again, but that all changed when Jason died.

I had never paid much attention to the house Mom liked, but Kate always said she hated it, because "it looks scary." It just looked huge and old to me.

I wasn't surprised when Dad got home from work the next afternoon and Mom was ready with all the information about the house she wanted. Two months later, we moved. That was real hard on our family, but I don't think Mom ever regretted it. To her it was worth the short tempers and all the work of moving.

Kate still thought the house was scary, but I loved it. It had twice the number of rooms we had in the country, and it was three stories high, plus a full basement, though not much yard. Mom and Dad talked Kate into sleeping in a room right next to theirs, and I had my own room upstairs with lots of places to explore.

13

We were still close enough to my school and even closer to our church, so I didn't have to get used to new people—except for a few neighborhood kids. Dad still thought the move was a mistake, but there's nothing he wouldn't do for my mom when she really wanted something.

I didn't think Mom looked much happier. She still cried a lot and spent a lot of time just sitting by herself. But most of the time she was busier than she would have been in the country. With a new house, she often said, there was always something to do.

I couldn't wait for my best friends to come see the new house. We'd have fun in it. But Dad didn't think four more boys in the house was such a good idea with Mom still sad and everything. I pouted for a while, which he told me was childish. But he also tried to make up for my disappointment by asking if I wanted to ride along with him on patrol the next Friday night.

That was something Jason hadn't done until he was fourteen, just before he got sick. I was so excited I started hollering, but Dad shushed me and reminded me that it would be only for a couple of hours. "I'll have you home by midnight," he said.

That sounded great to me. I wasn't ready for Mom's reaction.

The Argument

I hardly ever heard my parents argue before we moved. They disagreed, sure. But they never yelled at each other or said mean things. I knew that was unusual because I'd been in enough friends' homes to know how most people talk to each other.

It had been real hard on both of them when Jason was so sick, especially when he was in the hospital for almost a year and they had to trade off visiting him and all that. When he came home for the last six months or so, Mom spent a lot of time crying, though never in front of Jason.

That had to be hard on Dad, because he always tried his best to be brave for her. It couldn't have been much fun having a wife who just cried all the time. But who could blame her? I'm sure Dad wanted to cry too, but he didn't very often. Somebody had to be strong, and I guess he figured he was the one.

Well, when I started bragging to Kate, in front of Mom,

that Dad was going to take me on patrol with him, she panicked.

"We'll see about that!" she snapped, and because Dad wasn't there to back me up, I started right in with my arguments.

"Oh, Mom!" I said. "Dad said I could, and he promised! You can't make him change his mind now! It wouldn't be fair!"

"Life isn't fair," Mom said. "Your father and I will talk about this, but I want you to know I'm against it. So don't get your hopes up."

"My hopes are already up," I said. "I'm counting on this! I need this!"

"Need?" she said. "You don't need anything you haven't already got."

I know she wasn't trying to be mean, but that hurt. I wasn't saying they didn't take care of us or that we went without the things we wanted and needed. But no one seemed to think that the last two years had been hard on Kate and me too.

I ran upstairs to my room, fighting tears, and flopped onto my bed. I wanted to pray that God wouldn't let Mom change Dad's mind. But that didn't sound like the right kind of a prayer, so I just buried my face in my hands and felt guilty and hoped and wished as hard as I could.

It didn't take long to get bored, so I went looking for Kate to show her my latest discovery.

"I don't want to see anything scary," she said.

"Quit being a baby!" I said. "I promise not to lock you in anywhere or turn off the lights or anything."

"I don't want to see the attic again—or that big closet in your room!"

"This is better," I said. "I think you'll like it."

I was wrong. I had found a sliding door in the wall behind my bed that led to a cramped storage area. It was too low to

16

stand up in, but you could scoot along to another sliding door in the wall at the other end of the room. I reached in and pulled a chain, and the light came on.

"I'm not going in there," Kate said, shaking her head and making her light brown hair bounce. "I'll get stuck."

"No, you won't. Now go on!"

"No! I'm afraid, and I don't want to be in there. Mom won't let you play in there anyway. I bet she'll use it to put blankets and stuff in."

"Not if I don't tell her about it," I said, knowing immediately that Kate would tell.

"You have to tell," Kate said. "No family secrets."

"Just go in," I said. "We can pretend it's a playhouse."

"I don't want to. It looks cold and dark in there."

"I turned the light on!"

"I'll get lost!"

"There's nowhere to go!" I said, frustrated with her. "You've got to grow up and quit being such a baby. It's just a cool place. Check it out."

"You go first."

"OK," I said, muttering under my breath about what a sissy she was.

Of course she hadn't promised she would follow me. Once I got in there, all crouched down and unable to turn around, Kate leaned in and said, "I'm going to tell Mommy you called me a baby!"

"I wasn't calling you a baby!" I said, trying to back out and hitting my head on the light bulb. But she was gone.

"Kate!" I shouted, coming out and sliding the door shut.

Kate was scampering down the stairs.

I knew I had to follow, just to defend myself. This was all I needed, with Mom already against my going on patrol with Dad.

By the time I got downstairs I heard Kate gushing the news. ". . . called me a baby and tried to get me to go into a

17

place in the wall that he wasn't gonna tell you about and—"
I interrupted and tried to explain.

Mom didn't want to hear it. "Toby, you know you're not to boss her around, and you also know she's particularly sensitive just now, don't you?"

I nodded. I had been told enough times. Why didn't anybody think *I* would be sensitive now too?

"I thought she might like to play house in there with her friends and with her dolls," I said.

"He never said anything about that, Mommy!" Kate said.

"You never gave me a chance. I'm not going to let you now."

"Why? I want to!"

"Oh, sure! You get me in trouble for showing it to you, and now you *want* to play in there!"

"Toby!" Mom shouted. "Enough! Go to your room. I'll come and look at the area myself and decide whether anyone can play in there. For now, just stay in your room until your father gets home."

I wanted to argue, but I knew it wouldn't do any good. It seemed to me Mom was being unreasonable and was taking Kate's side more now than she used to. I knew it all had to do with Mom still being so sad about Jason. I was sad too, but I was tired of nobody understanding what I was going through.

A few minutes later I dropped onto my bed again and lay on my back, staring at the ceiling. Kate was all right. I wasn't really mad at her. Just frustrated. She was cute and funny and everybody loved her. I thought she was spoiled, and I knew I was too. But she'd always been the only girl in the family, everybody's little angel.

Jason had been the handsome, smart, oldest child. He was responsible, whatever that meant. He did big chores, had a paper route, and got good grades. He was also a good athlete.

People told me I was better at sports that he had been at my age, but nobody would care until they saw how I did when I got to be his age. I had just started showing what a good basketball, soccer, and baseball player I was when Jason got sick. It was hard to admit that I resented it when Mom and Dad couldn't come to as many of my games because of him. I knew they didn't have any choice. But it still seemed to me as if I had disappeared for a while.

I rolled onto my side and realized I was hungry. I couldn't wait until Dad got home for dinner and we could settle this patrol thing once and for all. Why wouldn't Mom want me to do it? It would not be on a school night, and it wouldn't last that long.

Through the register in the floor I heard a door open and then Kate's voice. "Are you taking a nap, Mommy?"

"No, honey. I'm just resting for a few minutes now that dinner is on the stove."

"Can I help fix it?"

"No, thanks. Be sure not to touch anything in the kitchen. The table's already set. You can help me with the dishes later."

"It's Toby's turn."

"Well, I thought you wanted to help."

"Not with the dishes! With dinner!"

And Mom actually laughed. I hadn't heard *that* in a while.

I was amazed I could hear them so well through the heating vent, but it made sense. My room was directly above Mom and Dad's. That meant they could hear me too. I'd have to remember that. I crept out of bed and lay on the floor, pressing my ear to the cold, metal opening.

"You want me to leave you alone, Mommy?" Kate asked, and she sounded as clear as if I were in the room with them.

"You can stay if you're quiet," Mom said.

I heard the bed creak as Kate joined her. "Can I just say one thing?" she asked.

"Um-hm," Mom said, sounding almost asleep.

"I love you, Mommy."

"I love you too, Katie."

"Not Katie! Kate!"

"You're my little Katie," Mom said, teasing her.

"No, Mommy! I'm Kate! And I'm not little."

They were quiet for a while, and then Kate said, "Mommy, we miss Jason, don't we?"

Mom sighed, and I heard her voice grow thick. "More than I can say, Kate."

I climbed back onto my bed and lay face down on the pillow, crying. I didn't know if my tears were for Jason or for Mom. Everybody said there was no more reason to feel bad for Jason. He was in heaven. I believed that, but it still hurt to think about him. I felt so bad for Mom, but I also wished she would at least act glad that Kate and I were still there.

I was dozing when I heard Dad pull into the driveway. I was down the stairs and out the door before he was out of the car. He was in his uniform, his bulletproof vest making his chest look bigger and thicker than it was. And it was plenty big and thick anyway.

Dad had his own weights and was always working out at home. He said that because he had just barely reached the height requirement to become a sheriff's police officer when he was twenty-one, he had to make up for that in other ways.

Lots of the other county sheriff's police were tall and heavy, but Dad had thick forearms and big muscles. He was trim and fit, the fastest runner, and the best pistol shot. I was so proud of him I could burst sometimes.

"Dad," I said, walking with him to the house, "Mom says she's against me going on patrol with you, and—"

"Oh, Toby, I wanted you to let me talk to her about that first. You know she doesn't like surprises."

"Well, I was telling Kate, and Mom overheard. I can still go, right?"

"No promises."

"Dad!"

"Toby, this is your fault. You should have kept quiet about

it. I see no reason why you shouldn't be able to, but—"

"Oh, good!"

"But I'm not your only parent. I will hear her out, and then we'll decide together."

"But Dad, you're the boss, aren't you?"

"Toby, you know I don't work that way. Your mom and I are a team. We come to agreements."

At dinner I brought up the subject so they would be forced to talk about it.

"We're going to discuss this in private, Toby," Dad said.

"Which we should have done in the first place," Mom said, giving Dad a cold look.

"Hon, I'm sorry," he said. "I *was* going to talk with you about it before Toby mentioned it, but—"

"But you already said he could go."

"Yes, but I didn't see any reason why he couldn't, and—"

"You *didn't?*"

The argument would have begun. Worse, it would have been my fault. But Dad was good at this kind of stuff. He knew what to say and how to say it to keep a bad thing from getting worse.

"I messed up," he said, taking Mom's hand and looking her in the eye. "We've both had a long day, and for hours I've been looking forward to a quiet meal with the family. This is great. Let's enjoy it, and you and I will talk about this later. You can ground me or not allow any TV for a week or whatever I deserve, but let's postpone the discussion till later, OK?"

Mom had to smile.

I almost did, but—if I had to guess—I thought my chances of getting to go with Dad on patrol were pretty slim. I just hoped they had their discussion somewhere close to a register that would pipe it into my room. I sure hadn't been invited, even though I was the subject they would be talking about. What else was new?

The Discussion

For an hour after Kate had gone to bed in the room next to Mom and Dad's downstairs, I sat in my bedroom finishing my homework.

Everything in school seemed easy for me except science. My teacher and my mom thought I had a mental block. All I knew was, I liked and understood all the other subjects. Science I really had to work at, and the only thing that seemed to work was to just try to memorize everything. I was pretty good at that because we'd been memorizing Bible verses in Sunday school for as long as I could remember.

I was putting my stuff away and about to say my prayer when I heard Mom and Dad talking. I could hear the TV news in the background, so I knew they were in the living room. I got into bed and lay very quiet.

Dad was apologizing for not having talked to Mom before inviting me on patrol. "I was going to mention it, but I didn't think it would be a problem."

"Well, it *is* a problem, Phil. I worry enough about *you* without having to worry about Toby too."

"You know you don't have to worry about either of us, Lynn. I'm not really on patrol when I'm out at night. I'm just backing up the beat officers. I'm a supervisor. I would never be the unit assigned to a dangerous situation."

"So you wear that bulletproof vest for what—to protect you from flying pencils in the office?"

It wasn't like my mom to be sarcastic, but she hadn't been her normal self for a long time.

"It's just a precaution, Lynn. You know that. It's been years since I was even in a dangerous situation, and it's unlikely now. If I had Toby with me, I wouldn't even back up a suspicious call without dropping him off first."

Mom was silent, so he continued. "For years you never seemed to worry, hon. I know you were concerned, but it didn't eat you up. Even when I came home in the morning after working the graveyard shift, you'd be sound asleep."

"That doesn't mean I didn't pray all night."

"But you didn't! We used to talk about that. You said you had a sense of peace."

"And I did," Mom said. "But things have changed, obviously."

"They've changed only for the better, Lynn. I haven't drawn my gun in the line of duty for almost ten years. You know the real work is not like on those TV shows."

"Still, there's always danger. I'm grateful your work is mostly in the office. If I lost you, I don't think I could take it."

"You're not going to lose me."

So that was it. Mom didn't even like Dad being on the street if it meant another person in our family might die. That was understandable, but she should have known Dad would never let me get into a dangerous situation.

I wished he would! I'd have loved being with him when he arrested someone he had to chase or fight or handcuff or

24

hold a gun on or even shoot at! Maybe the guy would run past me, and I could trip him or kick him or do something to slow him down. Then I'd get a medal from the governor or something!

But I knew better. Dad just wouldn't let that happen. And who knew if I'd be that brave when the time came anyway?

"So I can't talk you out of this?" Mom was saying. "You've made up your mind?"

"It's not like that," he said. "I personally think Toby would be as safe with me as he'd be here with you. It's as unlikely that anything would happen to him on routine, supervisory patrol as that someone would break in here or that a fire would break out."

"What pleasant thoughts," Mom said, sarcastic again.

"Lynn, we have to think of Toby here too."

"Who do you think I'm thinking of?"

"I'd rather not say."

"Philip! What are you saying?"

"Lynn, you know I've tried to be understanding. We're all devastated over Jason. I didn't know it would be this difficult for this long for both of us, but it is, and we have to deal with it. But we can't make the other kids suffer by overprotecting them."

"Is that what you think I'm doing?"

"Of course you are. I understand. And I don't blame you. I can't imagine losing another child either, but what kind of a life are we going to give them if we keep them locked away from their friends or the outside world? You realize Toby hasn't had his friends over even once during this school year?"

"I thought you agreed with that."

"I did for a while. And I still think there need to be limits. But at least let me get him out of the house so he can have some fun and do something different."

"Then take him to a ball game, the circus, a concert,

whatever. I'd rather he have his friends over, if that's what it would take to keep his own father from exposing him to dangerous criminals."

"I wouldn't expose him to criminals! He wants to see what I do, where I work. It'll be good for him to know that it's not all action and drama. Police work is also routine and full of paperwork. When I was his age I was fascinated by it all anyway. He needs the right to decide what he thinks about it after seeing it from the inside."

Mom was silent again.

I was rooting for Dad, of course, but I felt bad for Mom.

"You think I'm thinking only of myself," she said.

"In a way, I do. I know you're thinking of Toby's welfare, but you said yourself you couldn't bear thinking of anything happening to one of us."

"Well, how about you, Phil? How would you feel? Especially if it were your fault?"

I was afraid Dad wouldn't have an answer for that one. But he did. "That's the very reason I would not put him in a dangerous situation, hon." He chuckled. "I'd have to answer to you."

I wished I could have been down there to see if Mom at least smiled. They were quiet, and I just hoped they were hugging. They used to do that all the time. Now it was usually just Dad hugging Mom, trying to comfort her.

"I don't think it's selfish to not want to lose another child."

"I didn't say it was selfish, but I want you to see that the issue is you as much as it is Toby's safety. Should I be insulted that you think I wouldn't protect him with my own life?"

Dad probably knew that was the wrong choice of words as soon as they were out of his mouth.

"Oh, that's all I need," Mom said. "Losing you so I won't lose Toby."

Sometimes I could hardly stand the way adults argued. They never seemed to get anywhere. All I wanted was for Dad to talk Mom into letting me go. Then I could start daydreaming again about disarming some bad guy and helping Dad put someone in jail. If Mom had known I was even thinking about that, it would have been the end of their conversation for sure.

It sounded as if Dad stood and began to pace. That was sometimes how he signaled that he was coming to some sort of a decision. "Here's what I think, hon. If you're still so fragile that you simply can't live with my taking Toby to headquarters and out on the street for a couple of hours, I won't put you through it."

"So it would be my fault if he doesn't get to go."

"Well, yes. But I think you should let him. I'll show him around the place, we'll ride around in the car awhile, listening to the calls, maybe backing up a traffic stop or two. Then I'll have him home by midnight."

"And if you get into a situation you can't get out of? Some emergency where you have to take action right away?"

"Lynn, that just so rarely happens—"

"Humor me. What if it does? What will you do if you don't have time to drop Toby off here at home or back at headquarters?"

"Then I'll make him lie face down on the floor in the backseat until it's all over."

I was sure Mom wasn't going to go for that. She knew as well as I did that I wouldn't want to be hiding when the good stuff was happening. But I guess Dad had said what she wanted to hear.

"I'm still not happy about this," she said. "And you know I won't sleep until you're both home."

"You're doing the right thing," Dad said.

"I hope so."

I could hardly sleep. How was I supposed to wait for Dad

to tell me I could go without letting on that I already knew? I prayed for Mom, I thanked God for a dad like I had, and then I dreamed of being a hero. Wouldn't it be cool to help my dad—or even save his life? How could Mom be mad if that happened? In my best dream it was a good thing I had gone on patrol with Dad, because he wouldn't have come back alive if I hadn't.

If that happened, Mom would want me to go on patrol with him all the time, just to protect him. I would become the youngest deputy sheriff in history and always be on the news. But those were just dreams. I knew better. If I was going to become a hero, it would have to be some other way.

Dad being in charge of scheduling, he assigned himself the 3:00 in the afternoon to 11:00 at night shift that Friday. He had an hour off from 6:30 to 7:30, when he would come home, pick up Mom and Kate and me, and take us out for a quick dinner. We hadn't eaten out in so long that I had almost forgotten how good and fun that could be. Then, after dinner, he would take me back to work with him.

Dad told me Friday morning that Mom was still against the idea. "Doing this family thing first will include her a little," he said, "and I don't want you acting like you won and she lost."

That made sense. The only problem was that I pushed my luck. I asked Dad if I could invite a few friends along—just the four guys I ran around with at church.

That made Dad mad. "If you knew what it took for me to make this all right with your mother, you wouldn't be asking," he said.

"OK," I said. "I was just wondering."

"You didn't say anything to them about it, I hope."

"Well . . ."

"Toby!"

"Well, Dad, I thought it was a sure thing, and I wanted them to know about it."

"What would have happened if you hadn't been able to go?"

"I didn't even think about that. I didn't know Mom would have a problem with it."

"You didn't actually *invite* anybody, did you?"

"No, but I'd sure like them to come and see the house sometime soon."

"So would I."

"You would, Dad?"

"I know this has been hard on you, Toby. You and those four guys had a lot of fun out on the ranch."

"That's been a long time, Dad. I mean, I get to go to their places once in a while, but I'll bet it's been almost a year since they came to see me."

"You've been good about all this, Toby. I know it's been hard."

"I'm glad somebody noticed."

"What do you mean?"

"Just that it doesn't seem like Mom thinks anybody should be as sad as she is about Jason."

"Someday you'll understand the unusual bond between a mother and her child."

"Don't you have the same bond? Don't I?"

"I'm sure there's very little difference," Dad said. "But you know mothers carry their children for nine months and then literally deliver them from their bodies. Mom would never say that she feels worse about losing Jason than I do, but I don't think anyone but a mother can understand that special attachment between a mother and her children."

I knew he was right, but I didn't know what I thought about all that. It still seemed as if I was being treated like a child. But I had feelings like anyone else. I was twelve, almost thirteen, not five or six. I was pretty sure my friends would understand, but they were too embarrassed about Jason to even bring up the subject. "Do you think when I see the guys on Sunday I could invite them over for next weekend?"

"We'll see."

"Here we go again."

"Don't be a smart aleck, Toby."

"I'm not, Dad. I'm just getting tired of everything being such a big deal. I used to have the guys over all the time. When are things going to get back to normal?"

Dad didn't say anything right then, but he must have agreed.

That night while we were out to dinner with the family, everyone seemed in a good mood for the first time in a long while. Dad started talking about some of the funny things I had done with my friends, and even Mom was remembering and laughing.

By the time we were through with dinner, it was agreed that I could talk to the guys Sunday and invite them to spend next Friday night at our new house and stay through Sunday morning.

I couldn't believe my luck: Friday night patrol with Dad and the next weekend with the guys. Of course I had to get all my homework done first, but that would be a small price to pay.

As Dad and I dropped off Mom and Kate at home, Kate was whining about not getting to go on patrol with us. Mom told her she could watch her favorite cartoon video. That seemed to satisfy my sister, but Mom was not happy. She must have been thinking more and more about my being out in a squad car in the middle of the night.

Headquarters

The Kalamazoo County Sheriff's Police headquarters my dad worked out of was a one-story building with offices, a two-cell jail, a communications center, and an area where suspects were fingerprinted and photographed. Downstairs was a pistol range for target practice.

I especially liked the communications center. The computers were glowing with information, and a couple of officers answered the phones. Someone else sat behind a command microphone, directing the squad cars. Dad showed me where the emergency 911 calls come in and how they are handled. He showed me a computerized map that revealed the locations of all the squad cars at the same time.

It made me proud that the people at headquarters treated my dad with respect. I knew he was their boss, but you can tell when people really like somebody and when they're just being polite because they have to be. I also enjoyed looking at all the trophies from the state pistol shooting matches and seeing how many had been won by my dad.

He showed me the locker room where the officers change in and out of their uniforms. Just when we were going in there, an officer was strapping on his gun and ammunition belt, which also had a place for his nightstick and handcuffs. I liked the way the leather squeaked.

The sounds and smells of my dad's squad car and his belt had always made me want to be a deputy sheriff too. It all seemed so cool, having everything you needed on your belt or in your car.

After showing me the pistol range and letting me shoot his gun once (it was too loud and ugly sounding; I didn't like it), Dad fingerprinted me just for fun, then he took a mug shot of me with a board chained around my neck that told my name and a pretend prisoner number.

I tried to look real mean, but just before he shot the picture, I burst into laughter. So my mug shot doesn't make me look very dangerous.

Dad paper-clipped a couple of dollars to a petty cash voucher and dropped it into a basket. I asked him what that was about.

"That's how we pay for personal use of office equipment," he said.

Nobody would have much of a problem with the deputy sheriff using one shot of the instant camera to shoot his kid, but Dad always wanted to do the right thing.

Then he threw me in jail. Well, he didn't actually throw me. He said there were times when all police officers are tempted to push prisoners around, and sometimes some officers do that. But they're not supposed to. It isn't right, and it could get them into big trouble. He explained to me that everyone in our country is supposed to be presumed innocent until proven guilty.

"That's hard," he said, "especially when you catch somebody in the act of committing a crime. You know they're guilty, but they haven't been processed yet. They have to be charged and then indicted or found guilty. Then the authorities can sentence them."

He said that sometimes police officers get so frustrated at bad guys going free that they want to punish them a little themselves when they get the chance. "We have to resist that temptation," he said.

He left his gun in a metal locker outside the door and took me into the jail, putting his finger to his lips.

There was a smelly and scruffy-looking young man sleeping in one of the cells. "Drunk," Dad whispered. "He was caught driving while 'under the influence.'"

"Under the influence?" I whispered back.

"Of alcohol," Dad explained. "Half our traffic deaths are because of drunk drivers."

"Bet somebody wanted to throw *him* around a little."

"Probably. But we have cameras in here to protect prisoners from being mistreated." He pointed up into the corner where a camera swept the area.

I waved, the way kids do to the cameras at big league ball games.

"Why did you leave your gun out there?"

"Policy," he said, still quietly. "Just in case somebody escapes or starts a fight before they get locked up, you don't want to have a weapon they could get their hands on."

"Anybody ever try to fight you in here?"

"Sure. About ten years ago I was putting a guy in the cell, and I could tell he was about to try to make a run for it."

"How could you tell?"

"His body was tensing up as I guided him through the door. I casually let my hand slide down his arm and put gentle pressure on the back of his hand. As soon as he tried to spin away from me, I clamped down on that hand as hard as I could and stepped to his side. As he tried to get away, that caused his hand to snap back. If he had gone any farther, he'd have broken it."

"Show me."

"OK, but be careful. I was leading him in like this. Now see where I'm holding your hand?"

"Yeah. That doesn't hurt."

"But try pulling away from me."

I stepped away from him, but that bent my hand behind me, and I couldn't move any farther.

"See?" he said. "I hardly have to do anything to get you to cooperate now. Shall I apply a little pressure to see if I can get you to walk with me?"

"OK," I said, not too sure.

Dad bent my hand back just a little, and I almost collapsed. He hadn't bent it far enough to even hurt me, but it seemed so unnatural that I knew if I resisted I could really hurt my hand.

"Cool!" I said.

"You want to be locked in jail?"

"Sure!"

He went back out to where he had left his gun and brought back the huge keys. "Do you trust me?" he asked.

"Of course. Why?"

"Because when I put you in the cell, I'm going to lock it and leave for one minute."

"OK. That'll be all right."

"Are you claustrophobic?"

"You mean afraid of enclosed places?"

He nodded.

"A little. I don't like being in dark closets with the door shut. This is big enough."

"I'm just saying, Toby, that this is going to be the longest minute of your life. But I promise I'll be back for you in sixty seconds."

"OK."

He unlocked the door, and I stepped inside. When he shut the door it was just like on TV when you hear a jail cell clang shut. There's something scary and final about it.

"You all right?" he asked.

"'Course!"

"I'll be back." He glanced at his watch as he left.

I stood there listening to the heavy breathing of the drunk guy in the next cell. What would I do if he woke up and started talking? I sat on the cot, which was hard and uncomfortable, and I wondered how anybody could stand using the combination toilet and sink.

For a few seconds I imagined bragging to my friends about being in jail, but soon it seemed Dad had been gone long enough.

I put my hands on the bars, just like prisoners are always shown doing, and was surprised at how solid everything felt. There would be no breaking out of a cell like this. Hadn't it already been a minute? In fact, hadn't it already been two or three?

I heard nothing but the drunk guy's breathing and the faint whine of the revolving video camera up in the corner. I waved at it again and tried to smile, feeling stupid. Maybe Dad was watching and would know I had had enough.

But what if he had gotten a phone call and no one was available to tell me it would be another minute or two? What if it was an emergency and he had to go and had forgotten I was in there? No one else would know where I was, unless they were watching that video monitor. But I had seen no monitor. Maybe this was just recording for future use if they needed it.

Now for sure it had to be five minutes, maybe more. I wondered if that video camera had sound. I called out softly. "Dad? You can come back now."

"Wha—?"

It was the drunk guy from the next cell. He stirred and sounded as if he was getting up. I heard him grab the bars of his cell. "Who's in here?" he hollered.

I backed up so he couldn't see me, and I held my breath. *Dad! Hurry!* I knew the guy couldn't get to me, but I didn't want him talking to me or even knowing I was there.

He swore. "Hearin' things again," he mumbled, and I heard him sit on the floor.

Where was Dad?

I was starting to panic. Now I was sure my father had been called away and had forgotten about me. I wouldn't be hungry until morning, but who knew when anyone would come in and check on the cells? There was no blanket or pillow. I wanted to holler, to call out for my dad, but I didn't want that drunk guy to hear me.

Just then Dad breezed in. "Fifty-nine, sixty!" he said, looking at his watch and smiling. "Was I right? Was that the longest minute of your life?"

I nodded, eager to get out of there.

"You want to stay in another minute, just to see what it's like?"

"No way! Get me out of here!"

"Who's t'other perp?" the drunk guy slurred.

"Nobody," Dad said. "Just sleep it off there, Rudy."

"You know him?" I asked as we left.

"He's one of our regular customers," Dad said. "We all know Rudy."

"What was he saying?"

"He wanted to know who the other perp was. That's short for *perpetrator.* Criminal. He just wondered who his jail mate was."

"Yuck."

"You didn't like that very much, did you, Toby?"

"No!"

"It's pretty ugly being locked up, isn't it?"

"Dad, was it really only sixty seconds?"

"On the dot."

I could hardly believe it. "Can we go on patrol now?"

"You've seen everything you want to here?"

"'Cept your office."

That didn't take long. I had been in there before. He had new pictures, one of him with the governor.

I was ready for some action. I hoped there would be all kinds of dangerous calls, but I didn't want to have to talk to any criminals. I was still shaking over that drunk guy trying to talk to me. I was ready to help Dad arrest somebody or wrestle people to the ground and cuff them, as long as I didn't have to ride with them in the squad car or talk to them. I knew none of that would actually happen, but it was fun to dream about being a hero.

I had always loved the squad cars. Dad never let me in his when he wasn't around. Of course, he didn't leave it unlocked. He said all the equipment they carried made them cost twice as much as a normal car.

Dad's squad car had a plastic divider between the front and back seats, in case he ever had to carry a prisoner by himself. It also had a police radio, a citizens' band radio, an emergency network radio, a cellular phone, and a computer with a screen and keyboard, hooked up to the state capital for checking on license numbers and stolen cars. A shotgun was also locked into place. I hardly had room to squeeze into the passenger's side of the front seat with all that stuff attached to the dashboard.

"This is like an office in a car," I said.

"Exactly," Dad said. "Let's roll."

He checked the flashing red light, then the siren with a short burp. He checked all the radios and asked if I wanted to tell the dispatcher that we were in service.

"How?"

"Well, I'm 119, so we'll call you 119A. You just say, '119A to base.' When she answers, she'll say, 'This is base; go ahead, 119A.' And you say, '119 and 119A are 10-8.'"

"What's that mean?"

"That we're back in service. And then she'll say, '10-4, 119A.' "

"And what do I say?"

He chuckled. "Nothing. You could keep that up all night. Once somebody says 10-4, that means unless either hears anything else, you're both agreed on what's happening."

"I don't need to say 'Over and out' or anything like that?"

"Nope."

Dad showed me what button to push when I talked and said I had to let up on the button to listen. With the engine running and the radio on, I grabbed the microphone and held it up to my mouth.

Just as I was about to push the button, I heard other voices on the radio, and Dad held up a hand to tell me to wait.

The Chase

Dad and I sat waiting in his squad car while radio traffic crackled over the air.

"Any numbers between 111 and 119 are our cars," Dad said. "Sometimes the officers or dispatch will shorten them to just the last two digits."

I heard, "16 to base."

The dispatcher said, "Go ahead, 116."

"In pursuit of a motorcyclist south on Oakland Drive just past 94. Had him stopped for speeding, but as I got out, he took off. He's at about eighty miles an hour right now."

"10-4, 16. 118, did you copy?"

"10-4," came the voice of a woman officer.

"What's your 10-20, 18?"

"About a minute west of Oakland Drive on 94," she said. "I'll settle in behind 116."

"10-4. I show no units south on Oakland to help with a roadblock. Will check with local departments for assistance."

Dad turned on his lights and siren, and we flew out of headquarters. "You ready, Toby?" he said.

"For what?"

"Get on the radio and repeat after me. '119A to base.'"

The dispatcher hesitated. "Go ahead, 119A," she said.

Dad told me what to say. "119A and 119 are 10-8, and our 10-20 is south of 94 on Oakland Drive."

"10-4, 119A. 16 and 18, you copy?"

The woman officer said, "10-4," and the other just clicked his radio button.

"Advise as necessary," the dispatcher said.

As we raced toward Oakland Drive, Dad peeked at me and asked if my seat belt was on. It was. "Did you understand that radio traffic?" he asked.

"Not really."

"Car 116 is chasing a speeding cyclist. Car 118 is close by but behind. They're both in pursuit. We're south of where they are, so he should be coming right at us."

"What will we do?"

"You never know till you get there," Dad said. "Cycles are the hardest to catch because they can go where we can't. I don't know what he's riding, but he can probably go across fields, unless he's on a big Harley. That would be a pretty rough ride."

"Should I ask him?" I said.

"Who?"

"Should I ask 116 what the guy's riding?"

"Sure, but we should be able to see him in a minute."

I think Dad was impressed when I radioed, "119A to 116."

"116, go," came the reply.

"What's this guy ridin'?"

"Small, quick dirt bike, didn't get a brand name."

"10-4."

"What's your 20, 119?"

I looked at Dad.

"He wants to know our location," he said, "our 10-20. Tell him we're two miles south of 94 on Oakland and ask him if he still has the perp in sight."

I did.

"Affirmative. I'll let you know if he leaves Oakland Drive."

"10-4," I said.

Dad was grinning, but he also looked determined.

This was great! He knew what he was doing, even if I didn't. He'd told me over and over that chases were rare, violence was rare. He'd always said the job was mostly driving around, being alert, talking to citizens, and doing paperwork. So I was lucky. My first time on patrol and we're heading off a speeding cyclist.

Over the radio I heard 116 ask 118 her 10-20. "You should see me in a second, 16," 118 said. "Soon as I crest this rise. I can already see your lights."

"10-4. Oh, there he goes. Took a right on the county road, now heading west. He's quick. I'm falling behind. 119, are you past where you can cut him off?"

We were just flying past an intersection when Dad heard that and slammed on the brakes. We slowed and then slid several hundred feet before Dad U-turned. "Tell 'em we're heading east, one mile south of the cyclist."

I radioed the information. "Tell us when to turn north again," I added.

"How did you know that was next?" Dad said.

"Give me some credit," I said. "If the guy takes a left, we've got to take a right to head him off."

"Good thinking. Why wouldn't he turn right and head back toward Kalamazoo?"

"Probably figures there's more chance of a roadblock there."

"Excellent, Toby."

41

We heard over the radio that 116 and 118 could see each other and both were guessing that the cycle would go south again at the next intersection about a half mile away. They were right.

"He's slowing!" 116 said. "He's turning right! No, left! He just swung right so he didn't have to slow too much."

I asked Dad, "What would you guess? Are we about a quarter of a mile west of where we can turn right onto the same road?"

"Exactly. Tell 'em."

As I was about to push the button, 116 asked our 10-20. I told him.

"We're behind him," 116 said. "See if you can keep him from getting around you."

Dad floored the accelerator, and I noticed we were traveling more than a hundred miles an hour. When he took his foot off the gas, we slowed quickly; then he gently braked, and we turned right.

I knew we would see the cyclist coming straight at us in just a minute or so. "Don't you want to turn your lights off?" I asked. "To surprise him?"

"Nope," Dad said, his eyes on the road. "I want him to think there's more than one of us here. He already knows he has at least one behind him. He made a big mistake already."

"What's that?"

"If he'd kept heading south on Oakland or west on the county road, he could have angled off into the fields and probably lost us. Look what he's got on this road."

I looked at the fields flying past in the night. "Fences," I said.

"Yup. Nowhere to go but around me on the shoulder, and these shoulders are pretty steep and soft."

"But you can't block 'em both."

"18 to 19, he just turned off his light!"

42

"10-4," I said, looking at Dad, who pressed his lips together and shook his head.

"He's going to be hard to see," he said. "I need to get crossways on the road and try to block whichever way he tries to get past, and I have to leave room for the other units to get past me too."

"You gonna try to shoot him?"

"No! We don't want to hurt him. He's probably not armed. Just scared and stupid. We want to stop him so he doesn't hurt himself or anyone else."

"So what're we gonna do?"

Dad slowed and stopped, maneuvering the car crosswise on the road, blocking both lanes. "Give me the radio," he said.

"I'll tell them, Dad!"

"Toby! Give it to me, now!"

I handed him the microphone. "19 to 18 and 16, I'm blocking both lanes, and I'm facing east. No matter which side he chooses to go around, I'll back up west and let you pass after he does. Any chance he's armed?"

"Negative. Helmet, but bare-chested. Never know what's in his jeans though. He's about a half mile ahead of me, so when you see my lights, he's going to be right on you."

"Keep watching, Toby."

I was watching, but I noticed Dad was on the side of the car that would be hit if the cyclist didn't go around us or stop.

"If you turned your lights off, he might hit us," I suggested.

"We don't want that, Toby."

"Should be within sight, 119," 118 said.

And I saw him. The flashing lights of Dad's squad car glinted off a tiny figure coming fast over the rise in the darkness.

"Duck down," Dad said.

"I want to see this!"

43

"Do what I say!"

I slid down a little in the seat, but the belt caught me, and I was glad I couldn't completely do what Dad had said.

Dad had his left hand on the steering wheel, his right hand on the gun in his holster, unstrapped. The cyclist had been able to see our lights for probably a mile, so he knew his only chance was to go around or give up. He had two squads behind him and who knew how many more on their way?

He seemed to slow and swerve, first to the right and then to the left, as if to see which way Dad would move. If Dad moved one way, the cyclist would try to scoot to the other shoulder. But Dad wasn't moving. He just sat there, tensed and watching.

Finally, when he was about a hundred feet from us, the cyclist accelerated, and I could hear the high whine of his bike as he turned on his headlight and angled left off the road to dip down onto the shoulder that ran in front of Dad's squad car.

"Oh, no," Dad said. "Big mistake."

I thought he meant the guy had found a way past and that we had made the mistake. But it had been the cyclist's mistake. The bike was bouncing and twisting, and unless he could straighten it out and get back on the road, he was in trouble.

My eyes were glued to the little bike as it came toward us in the ditch across the road. If he had been doing 80 or 90 miles an hour before, the loose dirt and rocks in the ditch must have slowed him to 50 or 60.

Suddenly, just before the bike swept past our headlights, the cycle hit a rut or a bump. And it was the coolest thing I'd ever seen—that bike went airborne, flying maybe fifteen or twenty feet. The rider flew off, and as the bike bounced and crashed and rolled and broke into pieces, he floated past us, right through the beams from our headlights, sailing toward the edge of a farmer's field.

"Oh, no," Dad said again. "Call dispatch for an ambulance and give 'em our 10-20."

But I couldn't take my eyes off the flying cyclist. One of his boots had flown off. He was wearing jeans and a shiny red helmet. He windmilled his arms as he soared down toward the fence. He just missed clearing the top wire, his remaining boot catching it and staying there as he flipped over and over and landed in the field.

"You're not going to want to see this," Dad said, as he grabbed his hat and his nightstick and jumped out.

"Oh, yes, I do," I said, as the other two squad cars slid up at crazy angles.

Dad leaned in and looked me in the eyes. "You stay right here," he said, "and call for an ambulance."

"Is he dead?" I said.

"Not if he's real lucky or drunk."

I would have to ask him later what that meant. He and the other two officers, all with guns drawn, leaped the fence. I radioed for an ambulance, then opened the door and stood on the edge of the floorboard to see what I could see. Nothing. I knew I couldn't leave the car, so I climbed out onto the hood and tried to see over the fence and into the field. Still no good.

I knew I might get in trouble, but I couldn't resist. I climbed onto the roof of the car and stood tall. From there I could see the burly biker lying face down in the dirt. Dad held a gun barrel to the back of his neck while the other officers searched his jeans.

"Just a wallet," the woman officer said.

"We've got to get his face out of the dirt in case he's breathing," the other said.

Dad holstered his gun and gently held the cyclist's helmet while the other two dug the dirt out from under his face. One lay his nightstick across the hole so Dad could rest the man's head across it and he could breathe without turning his head.

45

The biker groaned and said, "Oh, man!"

"Lie still, partner," Dad said. "Try not to move."

"I *can't* move, man!"

"You been drinkin' tonight, Dilbert?" Dad said, holding his flashlight on the license the woman officer had pulled from the wallet.

"A little."

"A little, huh? How much is a little?"

"A six-pack or so."

"Don't move, now. How are you feeling?"

"I don't feel nothin' at all, man. That's not good, is it?"

"'Fraid not, pal. This isn't gonna be one of your favorite memories."

But it was sure going to be one of mine.

The Guys

That Sunday at church I told my four best friends the whole story. We were standing in the foyer at church, waiting to go into the morning service after Sunday school.

They could hardly believe it. I told them how I scrambled down off that roof and was sitting in the car when my dad came back, and how I stayed there until the ambulance hauled the guy away. I also told them how for the rest of the evening, until Dad got off at eleven o'clock, everything about patrol was just as boring as he always said it would be.

"Did you get the lecture?" one of the guys asked.

"'Course," I said. "Dad asked me what I had learned from the chase. I knew exactly what he wanted to hear, and of course he was right. But it isn't like I didn't know that before. I told him it was stupid to drink, really stupid to drink and ride a motorcycle. It was dumb to speed in the first place and really dumb to try to outrun the police."

"Why was he so mad about you wanting to make that one radio call?"

"He said he didn't have time to say it and have me repeat it. The guy was coming at us at full speed, and he had to let the other two cars know what to do."

"What happened to the guy?"

"He was lucky. He bruised some bones in his neck and spine, but he didn't paralyze himself. He'll be on crutches for a few months, but he'll walk again. He lost his license. Can't even drive a car for a year."

"And what did your dad mean about him being either lucky or drunk?"

"Dad says that if someone's really drunk, they're less likely to be all stiff and tense when they get in an accident. That's why drunk drivers kill so many people and seem to walk away themselves."

Jonathan Bynum, the joker of our group, flashed his big goofy smile and shook his head, making his red hair spin out straight like a clown's. "So in other words, if you're gonna get in an accident, make sure you're good and drunk so you won't get hurt so bad."

We all laughed, but then I told them I had said almost the same thing to my dad. "He said that might almost make sense, except the idea is to avoid accidents, and the same booze that makes you relax is what causes the accident in the first place."

Jonathan saluted, still grinning. "I was kidding, Chief Andrews!" he said, and everybody laughed again.

The other guys wanted to know if my dad got in trouble with my mom for taking me along on a high-speed chase. "That guy could have rammed you two, and you could have got hurt."

"I know," I said. "It was great!"

"Did your dad not tell your mom, or what?"

"He doesn't keep stuff from her. He told her straight up what happened and said he was sure the whole time that I would be safe. She asked him how fast he was driving, and he told her. She wasn't too happy, but you guys can still come over next Friday night and stay till Sunday morning."

"Cool. Do we get to ride along with your dad on patrol, too?"

"No. I already asked. Sorry."

"Oh, man!"

"He will take us to the station house, though," I said. "You can see all the stuff and maybe get thrown in jail like I did."

I told them all about that and the pistol range, but I also told them Dad absolutely refused to even think about letting them shoot. "So don't even ask," I said.

The guys were excited about the next weekend. They wanted to know where we would meet. On the ranch we'd had a little shed we called our clubhouse. I told them about the storage area in the wall beside my bed, but I also said that would be too small for the five of us. "You can't even stand or turn around," I said.

"Well, where else?"

"We'll have to look, but it's a huge house. Maybe in the attic or the basement. Can you all be there by dinner time? Mom says we can cook out."

Jonathan lived close enough that he would ride his bike over.

Daniel Jackson, who was my age but a lot bigger and stronger, was a black kid with a round face, huge eyes, and teeth that looked too big for his mouth. My mom always said it was just typical of our age and that we'd all "grow into" our teeth. That sent me right to the mirror, and I was shocked to see that she was right. Daniel's teeth just looked more that way for some reason.

"My mom will drive me over," he said. He lived farther away, but we all told him to be sure and bring his bike. "Don't worry," he said. "I'm not gonna get stuck riding your sister's baby bike again!"

Thomas Christian was the quiet one in our group, but he was also our protector. He was the tallest, with curly black hair and dark eyes. His facial features were already defined, so he didn't have that junior high look. He looked like a man. I guess he had already grown into his teeth. He was thin and wiry, but he had muscles. I wouldn't have messed with him, and, with Thomas around, we didn't worry about anybody bullying us.

He was the only other one who went to my school, but he was in the other sixth-grade class. Thomas lived at a local home for boys and girls with no parents, and whenever he came over, my dad or mom had to call for permission, then go and sign him out and pick him up. We were responsible for him until we took him back.

Tom didn't smile much and was kind of suspicious of people. He was slow to get to know and for a long time he didn't much trust me or the others. But once I got him coming to church, he finally warmed up. He still didn't talk a lot, but you could tell he considered us his family. Whenever we planned to do something together, he was willing to come along.

The last member of our little group was Joel McBride, who was two years younger, small and skinny, a blond-haired kid with green eyes. He always looked dirty and scruffy, but he was so much fun that we enjoyed him. He claimed to hate girls, just as we all did, but you never saw anybody show off more when Kate was hanging around. Joel said he would check with his parents to make sure he could come for the whole time.

I always thought of my friends with titles. It was Big Dan, Little Joel, Old Tom, and Red Jon. We'd had some unbelievably fun times before Jason got sick and I could see the guys only at church. We used to run all over the ranch, exploring, hiding, playing war games, pretending to be sheriffs, anything you could think of.

Friday night wouldn't come soon enough. We planned to explore our new house, find a place to meet, and then start our own club.

"We've never had a name before," Red Jon said. "I think we should be the Five Stooges."

Big Dan laughed, unable to hide those huge teeth. "I think we should be Tom's Marauders. He's so scary, we can all look tougher if we line up behind him."

Tom pursed his lips and moved in front of Big Dan. Dan was probably heavier than Tom, but Tom was clearly taller and stronger. He was not smiling. He hardly ever did. Tom gently took hold of Dan's shirt and pulled him close. "What if I don't want my name used for our group?" he said.

Big Dan's smile froze. "I'm just kiddin', man!"

"So am I," Tom said, and we laughed so loud one of the ushers told us to hold it down.

After church we all met again to talk about the next weekend. I told Tom my dad would call the Home.

"So what're we gonna do?" he asked.

"Friday night cook out and then explore the house," I said. "Find a place to meet. Decide on a name for the club. Saturday morning my dad's gonna give us a tour of the sheriff's headquarters. Then we've got the rest of Saturday to do what we want. Sunday morning we all go to church. Dan, Joel, and Jon go home with their parents, and we run you back to the Home."

Tom nodded. "And we all agree my name's not gonna be in the name of the group?"

"Dan sure agrees!" Red Jon chortled.

The week sure seemed to drag. Every time I saw Tom at school he was either grumbling about his homework and saying he was a lousy student, or he was talking about the weekend. "I'm gettin' my homework done in advance," he said. "I don't want anything in the way of our fun."

"You're really looking forward to this, aren't you?" I said.

51

"Anything to get out of the Home," he said. "You can't imagine how boring it is with all those kids, watching some dumb video or playing games all weekend. I need a break. I thought we were never gonna get invited to your place again."

"I wondered myself," I said. "You're gonna like it, though."

"Are you sure? 'Cause I really liked the ranch. It was so open."

"Well, this is in a neighborhood, and the yard's not that big. Or, I should say, the yard is big, but the house is big enough to fill it."

"So there's no running or hiding outside?"

"Not really. But I hope my mom is up to having us run around the house a little."

"How about riding our bikes around the neighborhood?"

"It's not as good as out by the ranch, but, yeah, we could do that."

"It'll be fun no matter what we do," Tom said.

I couldn't imagine his saying that to anyone else about anything. The kids at school were afraid of him because of how old he looked and acted and where he came from. They thought he didn't care about anything or anybody. They thought he had an attitude.

The problem was, no one had taken time to talk to him, to listen, to get to know him. He wasn't a very happy kind of a person, but he cared about a lot of stuff. He wasn't a great student either, but he understood many things. My dad said he was street-smart. All I knew was that he had become one of my best friends.

When we first met, he was hanging around with another kid named Jim from the Home, a guy who had had polio and wore a brace on one leg. That made him walk and run awkwardly, and sometimes people made fun of him. Jim isn't still at the Home, but Tom used to defend him and beat up anybody who gave him a hard time.

Once I almost got caught in the middle. I saw some kids taunting Jim, and I ran to help. The kids turned on me but ran off when they saw Old Tom coming.

"Were those kids hasslin' you?" he asked Jim.

Jim nodded. He was big enough to take care of himself, but he couldn't catch anybody to make them pay for what they'd done.

Tom immediately jumped me, pulling me off the ground and demanding to know what I thought I was doing.

I was scared to death, but I couldn't find the words to defend myself. Jim hardly knew me, and I knew if he didn't speak up for me, I was in trouble. My safety was in Jim's hands.

"Not him, Tom!" Jim said. "He's cool. He was helping me."

Jim left our school soon after that, and Tom and I started hanging around together. He never said much. He didn't thank me for sticking up for Jim, and he didn't apologize for almost smashing me. He just sort of acted like he was sorry by being nicer to me.

Nobody was going to get anything soft or sentimental out of Tom. He did what he wanted and talked to whom he wanted. I was proud to be seen with him and be known as his friend. I could have told him how to be friends with more people, but he never asked. His eyes and his mind always seemed to be somewhere else. He wasn't the kind of guy you offered advice to unless he asked. And sometimes not even then.

When I finally got up the courage to invite him to church, he was more excited than I had ever seen him. He said his aunt used to take him to church, and that he was a Christian.

"They have some kind of services at the Home," he said, "but they're terrible." He explained to me how an adult had to become his temporary guardian if he left the Home, but that it could be done.

He didn't say much at Sunday school or church, but he surprised me by how much he knew about the Bible. I had to admit I had invited him to church to try to win a contest. And he admitted he started coming just to get out of the Home for a little while, so I guess we had been using each other.

But when all the other kids I brought quit coming, he still came. Now we were friends. He was still quiet and sometimes moody, slow to smile. But he was a good kid and a true friend. I was glad he was part of our little group, and so were the other guys.

It seemed as though Tom was sad, and I couldn't blame him. It had to hurt to see that the rest of us had parents and brothers and sisters. The thing that surprised me the most about Tom, though, was that somehow he found a way to get to Jason's funeral. My dad had enough to think about without having to arrange for that, and I don't think anyone even thought he would come. The other guys came with their parents, of course, but we were all shocked when Tom walked in. He was there with some worker from the home who had driven him.

He signed the guest book and shook hands with my parents and me and even Kate, but he never said anything. The next day we got a sympathy card from him. That said more to me about Tom than anything else ever could have. I didn't know if I'd ever hear his whole story, where he came from, what happened to his family, how he wound up at the Home, any of that stuff. I just knew I would be his friend for as long as he'd let me.

On Friday I saw him at lunch.

"Everybody still coming tonight?" he asked.

I nodded.

"Good," he said. "It's been a long time. We're gonna have some fun."

More fun than we knew.

The House

I was so excited about having all the guys over that I could hardly calm down. Mom and Dad were in the backyard barbecuing, and Kate was helping set the picnic table. Mom said I could show the guys around the house if we agreed to handle cleanup duty after dinner. That was a deal.

We charged through the house, running, hiding, jumping on beds and over the bannister, sliding down stairs, all that. If Mom had been inside I'd have probably been in trouble, but we didn't break anything. Every once in a while I'd peek out the window at the cloud of blue smoke billowing from the charcoal grill, and Mom would be wiping her forehead with the back of her hand and staring at the house with a worried look.

The guys and I raced up the stairs to the attic and climbed all through there, stepping over boxes and looking through my dad's old trunk. The attic was hot and steamy, though, and I didn't think my parents would let us use it as a meeting place anyway. A whole bunch of our stuff that Mom hadn't unpacked yet was jammed in there.

I showed the guys all the bedrooms and spare rooms, my mom's workroom, my dad's den, the parlor, a playroom, a TV room, a rec room.

"Man!" Jon said. "This is bigger'n where Tom lives!" Jon glanced at Old Tom to make sure he was not frowning.

He was just nodding. "I'd sure rather live here," he muttered.

Big Dan grinned. "Wouldn't we all? Let's check out the basement!"

We bounded down the steps, and I showed them the big old furnace that used to run on coal in the olden days. Then it was changed to be more modern, and now it was just there because it would have been too much work to remove it when the new, smaller furnace was put in. The old one was a big, scary-looking thing.

The five of us looked for a spot in the basement to turn into our clubhouse area, but nothing looked right. It was damp and cool, and we'd have had to do some building to make a place to meet. That would take too much time. I was sure my dad wouldn't want us messing with something that complicated anyway.

Suddenly we heard footsteps upstairs. Kate was running through the house, calling for us.

Little Joel's eyes lit up, though he would have denied it.

Red Jon said, "Let's hide!"

"I don't want to hide," Tom whispered. "I'm hungry. Maybe it's dinner time."

"Just for a minute," Dan said. "Where does this lead to?"

He stood by a door I had never opened. Dad had said it was the coal bin, which hadn't been used for decades. He said it probably still had coal dust in it that would get all over you.

"Coal bin," I whispered. "We could just step inside and shut the door. I don't think there's a light, but we could wait there till she comes looking for us."

"Yeah!" Dan said. "And then we could scare her!"

"We'd better not," I said. "I'd never get to have you over again. Let's just hide in there and then come out when she gets tired of looking for us."

We heard Kate calling, "Time to eat, boys! Where are you?" Her footsteps were in the kitchen, near the basement steps.

Dan yanked the door open, and coal dust flew out.

I felt around on the wall for a light switch and found nothing. The door would open only about eight inches, so we squeezed through one at a time.

As we gently pushed the door almost shut, it was all we could do to keep from bursting out laughing. We heard Kate coming and calling. The basement light was on, so she had to be pretty sure we were down there. It was hard to breathe in that little dusty room, and it was as black as night.

I held my breath as Kate came right past the coal bin door, calling our names. "Toby! Boys! Danny! Joel! Thomas! Jonathan! Dinner!"

We were pinching and tickling each other, fighting not to giggle and let on where we were. Finally Kate gave up and headed up the steps. We got in line to come running out of the coal bin, but as Kate reached the top of the stairs she flipped the basement lights off, and we were in pitch darkness.

That made us laugh our heads off, but we were still in the coal bin and now Kate couldn't hear us. We wrenched the door open and staggered around in the dark. Now I could hear Kate outside, telling Mom and Dad that she couldn't find us.

"Oh, Kate," Mom said. "They have to be in there. They're just hiding from you."

"No, Mommy! I looked everywhere!"

"Phil, find them, will you? We're ready!"

"We'd better get going," I said.

"Can we come back here later?" Joel asked.

"Sure, unless we get in trouble now."

We came around the side of the old furnace, and by the

faint light coming in one of the basement windows we found the stairs.

Just as Dad got to the back door, we came running out past him, laughing. Dad smiled as we flashed by.

But when Mom saw us, she looked horrified. "Oh, no!" she said. "Where in the world have you been? Look at yourselves!"

We rushed over to the windows to look at our reflections. We were covered with coal dust.

"Use the hose and get cleaned up," Mom said. "Don't even think about going into the house with that stuff all over you."

It was in our hair and on our faces and all over our hands and clothes and shoes.

Mom was pretty upset until Big Dan, waiting his turn at the hose, went over to her and smiled that grin of his. "Mrs. Andrews," he said, "do I have to hose down too? I don't see anything on me!"

"Oh, Daniel! I can see the coal dust even on you! Now git!"

Someday I was going to have to ask Dan if he knew why black people were called black people. If there was ever proof that they're not really black but actually all different shades of brown, it was when that coal dust got all over us. Daniel was actually a rich, chocolate brown, and that black dust showed up on him almost as clear as on us white kids.

We were all pretty pale except for Tom, who was kind of olive-colored. But Jon! With his red hair and freckles, his skin was as chalky white as it could be. Of course, we weren't actually white, any more than Dan was actually black. Dad had always said that everybody was colored just a little differently, and he'd be glad when nobody even thought about it.

That's the way we boys were. In fact, Daniel brought it up more than we did. We were all just friends. That's all we cared about.

I was glad Daniel had said that to my mom, though, because it seemed to loosen her up a little. She wasn't really ready to have a houseful of boys yet, but she was trying her best to let us have fun. I could all tell she was nervous and upset, and at first the guys didn't know what to say or how to act around her. Except Big Dan. He had said just the right thing, and all of a sudden even Mom was having fun.

Dad prayed, and we ate—way more than we should have. At least that's what Mom and Dad always say. It seemed just the right amount to me. Tom said they hardly ever had charcoal-grilled burgers at the Home.

And then he said something that made everybody look down or look away and clam up. Tom turned to my mom and said, "Mrs. Andrews, I'll bet it's at times like this that you miss Jason the most. I know I do. He would have loved just sitting here eating with us, wouldn't he?"

Man, I thought I'd heard everything! Even Dad seemed to freeze, wondering if this would bring on some kind of a crying spell with Mom. Kate just sat there chewing and finally looked at her. I had to too, wondering how in the world she was going to react.

But it was like a miracle. Mom set her burger on her plate and let her shoulders slump. She swallowed her bite and smiled. She sighed and shook her head. "That is for sure, Thomas," she said. "Jason loved picnics and having friends over. He was always good to you guys, wasn't he?"

Everybody chimed in, a little too loudly because the whole conversation made us nervous. But we insisted that Jason had been the perfect older brother, that he never treated me or my friends like pests, often gave us rides on the riding mower, and even played with us now and then—before he got sick anyway.

"He was a great guy," Dan said. "I miss him."

"So do I," Mom said, and she didn't even seem on the verge of tears. "Remember that time he taught you guys how to play a game with that plastic ball and bat—and none of you could hit a thing?"

Joel laughed. "I was only eight," he said. "I think I screwed myself into the ground swingin' at that thing!"

"Me too," Tom said. "Jason had taught himself some kind of a tricky pitch, and none of us could come close to it. Later he started throwing straight balls, just so we wouldn't feel like total failures."

"Yeah," Red Jon said. "Even I hit it after a while. Mr. Baseball!"

We all laughed, because Jonathan was the worst baseball player of us all. He was good in other sports, but not baseball.

Kate suddenly piped up. "But know what? I'm the luckiest, because he was my big brother!"

The others nodded.

"Hey, mine too," I said.

"Yeah, but I was his only sister," she said.

I laughed. "Think about it, Kate," I said. "I was his only brother."

"Yeah," she said. "But I had two brothers, and you only had one."

"Let's stop arguing," Dad said.

"We're not," Kate said. "We're just teasing. Just like Jason used to do."

"I know," Dad said. "Let's just be grateful for our wonderful memories."

"I want to say one more thing though," Mom said.

And we all fell silent again.

"I want to thank Tom for bringing up Jason. I needed to remember him when he was healthy and happy and enjoying his family and friends. It's hard to remember those days after two hard years."

She didn't break down. Her lip didn't even quiver. She was looking Tom full in the face.

He looked at her and looked away and looked at her again, red-cheeked. When he looked down at his plate, it was Tom who was fighting tears.

The Coal Bin

After dinner it started to get dark, so we boys had a contest to see how fast we could clear the table and get everything thrown away. Except for the times when two guys grabbed the same thing, we worked well together. Even though it got us all laughing again, we must have cleaned that whole area in less than five minutes. One thing we didn't want was to waste play time.

Kate kept marching around us, trying to act as if she wasn't bragging. But she said things like, "Well, my work's done for the day. I guess I can just do whatever I want."

"Then go do it!" Joel yelled at her.

He growled and chased her until she squealed and ran into the house. She knew he liked her, so she wouldn't tell on him. Mom eventually set her up with her own little project to keep her out of our hair.

We still had three hours to have fun before bedtime. Of course, we would still have fun after that, but we'd have to be quiet.

Once Mom inspected our work and told us we were free to do what we wanted, we all ran to our bikes. Tom didn't have one, of course, so he used Jason's old one. That was kind of weird, but there was no sense having it go to waste.

We raced through the neighborhood and then over to Tom's and my school. It was hard to ride on grass and dirt, but we pretended we were motocross cycle riders and laid out some race courses. Nobody could keep up with Tom. Jason's old bike was the best, and Tom seemed as strong as a man.

We got hot and tired and sweaty and rode home slowly in the dark, after stopping at the store for Cokes.

"What do you want to do now?" I asked.

The guys looked at me like I was crazy.

"What do you think we want to do?" Red Jon said. "We want to see what's in that coal bin that made us so dirty."

"It was coal dust, of course," I said. "I told you that."

"Yeah, but how big is the room? What's in it? It's cool!"

"There's no light in there," I said.

"C'mon, Toby," Big Dan said. "Get a brain. You've got flashlights, don't you?"

"Yeah."

"Enough for everybody?"

"Probably."

"You'd better have one for me," Joel said. "I'm not goin' in there without one."

A few minutes later we were home, digging through junk drawers and closets and my dad's workroom for flashlights. We came up with enough for everybody, but some didn't work and others didn't have batteries.

"I don't need one," Tom said. "I'm not scared."

"I'm not scared either," Joel said. "I just want to see where I'm going."

We all looked at him, smiling.

"OK," he said. "I'm a *little* scared."

We wound up heading down there with me in the lead

carrying a huge, five-battery flashlight and Big Dan bringing up the rear with a regular one. The others each carried one too, but only Little Joel's was working at all, and it was pretty faint. I don't know what the others were doing with theirs, but maybe they felt safer with some sort of weapon.

"Turn off the basement lights too," Tom suggested. "It'll be more fun."

"No!" Joel said, which made us all the more sure that was exactly what we wanted to do.

"You'll be safe, little buddy," Tom said. "There's nothing down there but monsters and slimy creatures."

We all laughed, but that made me shiver.

Dan shut the basement door and turned the lights off.

"Turn your flashlights off too," Tom said. "Let's see if we can find the coal bin in the dark."

"We have to use the flashlights once we get in there, though," I said. "Otherwise we're gonna get filthy again, feeling around the walls."

I turned off my light, but Dan held his up under his chin, making his big round face look like a pumpkin. He made all kinds of faces and noises, and Joel backed up until he bumped into me. When Dan finally turned off his flashlight, we could still see. Old Tom had hold of my belt from the back, Little Joel had his fingers in Tom's belt loop, Red Jon was doing the same to Joel, and Big Dan was last in line, hanging onto Joel's shirt.

Everybody turned and looked at Joel. His faint little light was still shining.

"Let's at least keep this on," he said, trying to sound brave.

"No way," Tom said. "Either turn it off, or we'll wait right here till the battery wears down."

"Which won't be long!" Jonathan said. "C'mon, Joel. Make some faces and then turn it off."

"Are you kiddin'?" Joel said. "And scare myself?"

Finally Tom traded flashlights with Joel. The one Joel got didn't work at all, but it was big and heavy, so he must have felt better with it.

Of course Tom immediately turned off the faint little one. We were in the dark again.

The five of us crept along the wall, with me in front.

"Don't we feel like a train of idiots chuggin' along in the dark?" Tom said, and I thought we were all going to fall over laughing.

"Feel that big old furnace," Jonathan said. "And tell what it feels like."

"I'm not touchin' it," Joel said.

"Come on!" Tom said. "It's time to grow up and quit being a sissy."

I heard him run his hand along the side of the furnace.

"It's not a furnace," he said. "It's a petrified octopus, and it's mad that we're here!"

"Cut it out," Joel said, sounding like he meant it.

Tom banged on the furnace with his flashlight and spoke in a low, rumbly voice. "Ooh, get out of my basement. Especially you, little one!"

Joel must have tried to break free and run. I turned on my flashlight just in time to see him nearly starting to cry. Tom had hold of him and was laughing, assuring him that nothing was here in the dark that wasn't here in the light. "Nothing can hurt you, man. We're just having fun."

Finally we were in the dark again, inching along the wall. I was feeling for the entrance to the old coal bin. Then I felt the handle and opened the door. "Hey," I said, "it's not as tight as it was."

"Must have been warped and scraping on the floor before," Tom said. "Opening and shutting it a couple of times loosened it."

We followed each other through the door. "Turn on a flashlight now," Joel said.

"Not yet!" Tom said. "Let's feel around and see how big this place is."

"Oh, man!" Joel said, and we knew he was just standing in the middle of the room doing nothing, waiting and hoping for some light.

I was puzzled because the walls didn't feel grimy and dusty like before. Then I came to some shelves! Why would there be shelves in a coal bin? And then I came to what felt like a circular saw blade, nailed to the wall. What in the world?

Suddenly the overhead light came on. Joel stood there grinning, happy and relieved to have found a switch. The rest of us squinted and shook our heads, realizing we were in a walk-in closet where my dad kept his junk. Did we feel like fools!

I had forgotten there was a closet next to Dad's workbench, and when you're moving in the dark, you have no sense of how far you've gone. I thought we were all the way across to the other side of the basement, but we hadn't even reached my dad's tools yet.

"Great explorers, aren't we?" I said. "That coal bin has to be twenty feet away."

"Lights off!" Old Tom commanded. "We're still gonna do this the right way."

"Oh, brother," Joel said.

"Why don't you go play with Kate, if you're gonna be a sissy," Daniel asked, turning the light off.

"He'd like that!" Jon said.

Suddenly I heard the door swing open, and Daniel yelped. "Who's there?" he said.

We all froze. He was the one near the door, and if he hadn't opened it, who had?

"I heard that," came Kate's squeaky little voice. "I'm not a sissy, and I'm not scared. I'll go wherever you guys go, and I don't need a flashlight."

"What're you gonna do now, Joel?" Jonathan asked. "Can't be a scaredy-cat if your little girlfriend isn't."

"She's not my girlfriend!"

"He's not my boyfriend!"

"Let's go!" Tom said, and our little train headed out again, this time with Kate.

As I felt along the wall, we came to Dad's workbench, the lathe, the table saw, the vise. Then there was the water heater, some ductwork from the new furnace, the humidifier, the washer and dryer, a utility sink, the freezer, a stack of bricks.

For a minute or so, no one said anything. We were moving slowly, hanging onto each other and feeling our way. I have no idea why that was so much fun, but it was.

Finally I came to the coal bin door—I was certain this time. And even with Tom helping, it was hard to get that door to scrape open past a few inches. He grabbed it, while the others waited behind us, and dragged it back and forth until the floor wore off some of the wood from the bottom. That way we at least got it open about a foot.

Once we had all filed in, Dan said, "Let me close this now."

We heard him shutting the door, and Joel said, "Just be sure we can get out of here when we want to."

"Why?" Jonathan asked. "You afraid?"

"Yeah," Kate said. "You afraid?"

"I'm not afraid!" Joel insisted.

"Me either," Kate said.

"Let's explore this room," Tom said. "I'll go around the right side with Kate and Joel. And Toby, you take Dan and Jon and go the other way. Don't race. Just feel along the wall, lightly enough so you don't get all dirty, and we should meet in the middle of the back wall. Then we'll guess how big the room is before we turn on the flashlights and see how close we came. Whatever you do," he added, "don't brush up against the wall with your clothes."

In single file, Tom's group went one direction and mine went the other. We were supposed to guess how big the room was by counting our steps.

"Hey, cool!" Tom said.

"What?" I called out.

"Can you touch the ceiling, Toby?"

"Are you kidding?"

"I can!" Tom said. "Try."

I reached up as far as I could and stood on tip toes. "Nope," I said. "Yuck! There's some cobwebs, though. Hope there's no spiders!"

"Me too," Joel said.

"I'm not afraid of spiders," Kate said.

"Me either," Joel said.

"If you can feel cobwebs, you're close to the ceiling," Tom said. "Remember, this was a coal bin, not a regular room. It wouldn't be very high."

"Well, you're taller than I am," I said. "That's why you can reach the ceiling."

"Hey, what's this?" Tom said.

"I give up," I said. "What's what?"

"I found some kind of a little door, right at the top of the wall on this side. It's maybe a foot and a half high and two or two and a half feet wide. It's on hinges. I'll bet I could open it! It feels like it opens to the inside."

We all stood and waited, listening to Old Tom fooling around with that little door he'd found.

"It's metal," he said. "I can't get it. Toby, come and help me."

"What makes you think I can open it?" I said, leaving the others and feeling my way to the other side of the bin. I bumped into Joel and made him shriek, which made Kate laugh. I tickled Joel, and he jumped away.

"Hey!" Joel said. "Quit it, Toby!"

"Uh-oh," Kate said. "I'll bet my clothes are black."

"I've almost got it," Tom said. "Just reach up and get your fingers under the ledge." In the darkness he placed my fingers on the bottom ridge of the hinged, metal opening. "Let's pull at the same time."

I put my flashlight in my pocket and reached up with both hands. It felt as if the door was about to give, but we really had to strain. Finally it creaked and broke free, flipping open and clanging off the ceiling.

With the little door open at the top of the wall, we could see outside. "I've seen this little door from out there!" I said. "It's next to the water faucet we use for the hose."

"That's what this pipe running along the wall must be," Tom said. "The water line."

Everybody crowded around the little opening and stared out at the stars.

The cool air felt good on my face. "This must be where they shoveled the coal in," I said.

"Well," Tom said, "let's shut it and keep going. I want to see what else is in here, but not till we've made it all the way around the room."

The Tunnels

Tom and I pulled the little coal-feeding trapdoor shut, and the room was black as night again. Our two teams of three people each went back to our places on either side of the room.

After we met at just about the middle of the back wall, we figured there would be nothing more to feel and we'd turn on our flashlights. Then we'd see how much bigger or smaller the room seemed in the light. We'd also try to see if we could use that little outside trapdoor as a way in. It would be too far to drop for the smaller guys, and Big Dan probably wouldn't fit through it, but it might be fun for the rest of us.

We edged along the wall in the darkness, somebody shrieking or making a funny noise or comment every few feet.

"We've reached a corner," Tom called out.

"Hold for a second," I said. "We're almost at our corner, I think. Yeah, there it is."

I knew my fingers would be black. And feeling my way

along was scary and made my neck tingle. Who knew what we might run across in the darkness? I kept imagining slimy creatures or a bat waiting to bite me. It was spooky and fun all at the same time. "Now let's see how close we can come to meeting at the middle," I told Tom.

It would be just a few more seconds now. Tom and I kept talking to each other as we moved closer and closer together along that back wall.

"Hey," Tom said, "I just reached some kind of an edge."

"Me too," I said, and you could tell from the sound of our voices that we were just a few feet apart. "It feels like some sort of trim, doesn't it?"

"Yeah," he said, tapping it with the useless little flashlight he had gotten from Joel. "It feels and sounds like metal."

"It *is* metal," I said. "You think we're pretty much in the middle of the wall?"

"Probably. Let's keep moving."

We edged closer until Tom and I bumped into each other and laughed.

"It's not a door," I said. "I don't feel any handle."

"Let me feel up and down the edges and see if there are hinges," Tom said. "If there are, it's a door of some kind. But you're right—there's no handle."

"You know what it feels like, Tom?" I said, as he edged past me, still running his hands up and down the metal edge, I guessed.

"Hinges!" he said. "What were you going to say?"

"It's not flat against the wall. It kind of bows out in the middle about a foot, doesn't it?"

"Yeah, so?"

"So, it feels like a bigger version of that coal-feeding door you found."

"You're right," he said. "Only it's vertical, not horizontal. The hinges were on the left side, so it has to open on the right."

"C'mon, you guys!" Joel pleaded. "Let's get a light on!

You're not gonna try to open some door to who knows where without seeing what you're doing, are you?"

"I can't think of anything I'd rather do," Tom said. He had taken the words right out of my mouth. "We just explored a boring, little room that turned out to be a coal bin with a feeder door in it. Big deal. Now we've found a door to something else, but to what?"

"I'm with Joel," Jonathan said. "Let's see what we've got here."

"Me too," Dan said.

"No lights yet!" I said quickly. "It's more fun to explore this without knowing where it leads. If anybody wants out, go ahead. Wait for us upstairs."

"I'm not leaving," Kate said brightly. "This is the most fun I've had in my whole life."

"Me too," Joel said.

"We're staying," Dan and Jon said. What else could they say when my eight-year-old sister wasn't afraid?

Tom and I ran our hands along the right edge of the big metal door. There was a gap of about a quarter of an inch, but we couldn't pry it open with our fingers.

"We're gonna need a big screwdriver or a chisel," Tom said. "Something like that."

I went back to get a couple of screwdrivers, just for fun not using my flashlight. I knocked into people finding the door, made a lot of racket scraping it open, then hurried through the dark basement, feeling my way past all the appliances until I got to Dad's workbench.

On the way I knocked on the old coal furnace and hollered at Joel, "Get out of my basement, little man!"

"Very funny," I heard from the coal bin.

I felt around for the screwdrivers and found two huge ones. I knew they would work. A minute later all I could hear was everyone else breathing as they waited to see if Tom and I could pry open that metal door.

We dug and twisted, but it was slow work. Every so often we heard a squeak that told us we were making progress.

"Man," Tom said. "I'm sweatin' like a pig. I think the door's stuck at the top and bottom both. It's like this thing is vacuum-packed."

It almost was. When we finally freed it at the right side and top and bottom, we were able to get our fingers in between the edge of the door and the metal casing. "Everybody help!" I said, and I could feel hands and bodies pressing together.

"On three!" Tom said, and he counted.

We grunted and tugged, and finally the door squeaked open and a rush of cold air hit us.

"Watch out," Tom said, as we swung the heavy door open all the way until it hit the wall.

I knew we were standing before an opening about the width of a normal door and probably six feet high. But where did it lead? And what was inside? Tom and I both hesitated, and I figured he was thinking the same thing I was. Neither of us wanted to admit he would rather see what we were getting into. It had been fun up to now, feeling our way through the darkness. But except for the surprises we'd found—the low ceiling, the coal-feeder trapdoor, and this big metal door—it was what we expected: a small, dusty coal bin.

One thing was for sure. Either we all went through that door, or none of us did. That was the way we had always done things.

"Are we in, or are we out?" I asked.

No one said anything.

"Well?" I said. "Who's going in there with me?"

"I will on one condition," Tom said.

I was shocked. It wasn't like him to be afraid. Was he going to insist on a light?

"We have to put something in front of this door to keep it open. If it shut us in, then what would we do?"

"I'll go get a brick," I said. "But while I'm gone, Kate has to decide if she's with us or not."

"I have to decide too," Joel said.

"Well, if you don't go, none of us go," I said. "It's all for one and one for all."

"But not for me?" Kate said.

"It's up to you," I said. "You don't have to if you don't want to. If all the guys want to go in, we go in."

"You going in in the dark?" Kate asked.

"No!" Joel said.

"Yes!" Jonathan and Dan said, and I was proud of them.

"What do you say, Tom?" I asked.

"Dark. And I say if Kate wants to go with us, Joel has to go."

"I'll go if she will," Joel said.

"But if I go," Kate said, "I want to be part of your club."

"We're not really a club," Dan said. "But I agree. If you're brave enough to do this, you're in. Everybody agree?"

I didn't hear anybody argue, and it was all right with me. Here was the little girl who didn't want to sleep alone after Jason's death, and now she was as brave as any of us guys.

I felt my way out to where I knew Dad had stacked a few bricks. One would hold the metal door open.

When I got back, we stood there in the blackness deciding who would go first. If I didn't know better, I would have thought Tom was nervous. He acted as though he was taking charge, telling everybody what order they would go in, but he picked me to go first. I was a little scared, but I couldn't back down.

"Let's go in this order," Tom said. "Toby, me, Dan, Jon, Joel, and Kate. OK?"

"And we're still going without lights?" I said.

Nobody said anything. With my dark flashlight in hand, I stepped forward carefully. The cool air from the opening in the wall gave me the chills.

Tom had his hand wrapped around my belt in back, and it was a good thing. I had no idea I was at the top of a stair. My second step took me out into no-man's-land, and I almost fell.

"Whoa!" I shouted, and Tom hung on, keeping me standing until my foot found the next step. "We're on stairs going down!" I said. "Careful!"

How many steps? Would they turn? There was only one way to find out. I slid my foot forward until it came to another edge, then I leaned back on Tom for balance as I stepped out into space, hoping the next stair would be the usual distance away. It was, and I was glad to find that after three steps I was on flat ground again. This would sure have been easier with light, but what fun would that be?

Our little train inched its way along for ten or fifteen feet, then hit a wall. The ceiling was only about five feet here, so most of us would have to duck to keep going. Cobwebs hung into my face and caught in my hair.

"When we gonna turn lights on?" Joel said.

"Never!" Dan called out.

Most of us laughed nervously.

I felt to the right. Solid wall. Nowhere to go. I felt to the left. Open space. "We're turning left," I hollered back. "Stay with me!"

"Like we're going somewhere else," Red Jon said.

I went another ten or twelve feet before my toes ran into something, and I pitched forward.

Tom tried to hang on, but I pulled him with me, and we both fell on some steps leading up. The rest just tumbled onto each other.

"It's just some more stairs!" I said, and everybody got back up.

Going upstairs was even trickier than going down. I had to feel my way with each step and lean against the wall for balance. I didn't know how low the ceiling was, and I didn't want to bump my head.

I finally came to a landing, but there wasn't room for all of us to stand there. I just said, "Stop! No more stairs, at least for a few feet here."

I inched forward and hit a wall. Had we come all this way to a dead end? "What do you make of this, Tom?" I said. "Feel this wall."

He edged past me on the landing. "No door or anything," he said. "No, wait! Yes, there is! Down here! A half door— low on the wall. Hang on a second," he told us. "We're gonna see if we can get this little door open."

"Will we fit through?" Jon asked.

"Yeah," Tom said. "We'll just have to squat. It's half a door. I found the knob."

He must have turned the knob. I heard the mechanism click. Tom and I pushed, but the door would barely budge. It was as if something was blocking it on the other side.

"Maybe we should go back," I whispered. I'd had about enough of this.

"No way," Tom said. "I didn't come all this way to give up. Come on, lower your shoulder into it and plant your feet. Everybody else back up a step and wait."

Tom and I put all our weight against the little door, and it began to move. Whatever was blocking it from the other side was heavy. We heard it scrape across what sounded like a cement floor, and it made an awful racket. We got the door open maybe six inches.

"Let's do it again," Tom said, so we pushed until the door hit the big, heavy object again. We pushed and pushed and budged it another few inches. I could almost squeeze through the opening now, but I wasn't sure I wanted to.

"Let's give ourselves just a little more room," Tom said, and we really grunted and groaned, heaving our bodies against the half door. Then what sounded like the scraping of wood table legs on the floor almost deafened us, and we stopped, sliding down to rest on the landing.

"I think we can get through there now," Tom said.

I was too tired to answer. I just nodded, knowing Tom couldn't see me.

"You goin'?" he asked.

Of course I was going. As he said, we'd come way too far to turn back now.

Junior Deputies

I was on all fours, crouching before the open half door. My flashlight was in my pocket. I leaned in and felt for solid ground. I didn't want to crawl out into the unknown and find myself falling. As far as I could reach, there was hard, cold, concrete floor. That was good news.

I reached around the door and felt for whatever it was that had been holding the door shut. I felt wood and steel, like a workbench similar to the one my dad had set up in the basement. I knew there was one like that in the garage. Could it be? Had we followed a tunnel from the coal bin all the way out to the garage?

I scooted through the door and gingerly stood up. If I was wrong, I didn't want to crack my head on another low ceiling. I slowly rose to full height and called for the others to come on in.

"What do you think?" Tom said.

"Garage," I whispered. I checked out the rest of the workbench—it was where my dad had stored more junk. Our cars couldn't be too far away. I moved and reached out to find them. Then, with all the mystery gone, I dug out my huge flashlight and turned it on. Joel, crawling in just ahead of Kate, looked relieved.

"This is too cool!" Big Dan said. "You can get to your garage from the basement. Too cool!"

I went and turned on the garage light. If I was as filthy as everyone else, I was a mess. Mom wouldn't be thrilled, but it had been worth whatever trouble I might have gotten into. We stood there smiling and breathing easier, everyone seeming as happy as I was that we hadn't gotten lost or trapped. And we hadn't run into any creatures either.

Everybody had cobwebs in his hair, but no one was complaining. In fact, no one was saying much of anything.

Kate piped up, "I came along! I'm in the gang!"

"We're not a gang," I said.

"Well, the club then," she said. "Let's go back the same way we came."

"Not so fast," Jon said. "Let's catch our breath. That wasn't easy, you know."

"Fear is exhausting," Tom said.

"I wasn't afraid," Jon said.

"Why weren't you?" Tom said. "I was. That's what made it fun." He nodded toward my flashlight. "Come on, let's see where we've been."

And we headed back down into the tunnel.

"Hey!" I said. "We've got to put this bench back in front of the door."

"We'll come around and do that later," Tom said. "It won't take half the time to get back in the light as it took to get here in the dark."

We followed him. It was hard to believe how short the route was down the stairs, through two tunnels, and up three steps into the coal bin. It took about a minute. When we got back there, we decided that little room—much smaller than any of us would have guessed—was the perfect place for us to meet.

"How will we ever get it clean?" Jon asked. "There must be years of coal dust here."

"It'll take a lot of work," Tom said. "But it will be worth it. What a great spot! We can go right from here to the bikes in the garage—and get here from there too."

We decided we would have to start with brooms and mops to get the cobwebs down, the walls and floor dusted, and then maybe get the place painted. We didn't know yet what form our club would take, but we knew what we'd be doing for quite a while—fixing up the coal bin for a meeting place.

While the rest went upstairs, Tom and I headed back to the garage to put the workbench in place. We went out the side door into the house from there.

That night in my room, after Dan and Jon and Joel finally fell asleep in their sleeping bags, Tom whispered, "Toby, did you see what I saw in the tunnels?"

"Something besides cobwebs, you mean?"

"There was a little opening off to the side, just before we turned to go up the steps to the garage. I felt it on the way out, and I sneaked a peek at it on the way back in."

"You think there's another tunnel?"

"Doesn't look like it. It just looked like a little storage area."

"So?"

"So you said you didn't think anyone in your family knew about the tunnels, right?"

"Right."

"Then they don't know about that little storage area."

"And?"

"And I saw something in there. Boxes or something. It didn't look like trash. It must have been something left there by whoever owned this house before you did. We ought to find out what it is and return it to them."

"Are you thinking what I'm thinking?" I asked.

Tom smiled. That was rare. I knew he wanted to go check out the storage area in the tunnels right then.

We grabbed the two working flashlights and crept out. It seemed to take as long to tiptoe down the stairs and avoid the creaks as it had taken to get from the coal bin to the garage in the dark when we didn't know where we were headed.

"Is this place closer to the garage or the basement?" I asked.

"The garage."

"Then let's go through the garage," I said.

We left the garage light off so we wouldn't attract any attention. Then we dragged the workbench away from the tunnel entrance and crawled through. When we got down the stairs and around the corner in the tunnels, there was the area Tom had told me about. It was about six feet square, and sure enough, it was stacked with boxes.

As Tom and I searched through the stash, we were stunned to see all kinds of auto parts. Neither of us knew much about car engines, but we recognized the brand names. Oil filters, carburetors, spark plugs, and even mufflers and brake pads filled the area. Two stacks of hub caps and wheel covers reached almost to the low ceiling. The stuff had to be worth thousands of dollars.

"Why would anyone stash this stuff here?" Tom wondered out loud.

"Maybe he worked at an auto parts store—or owned one," I said. "He probably just forgot this stuff."

"But why wouldn't he keep it at his store or in his garage, someplace where it would be easier to get to?"

"Maybe it needs to be out of the light."

"I never heard of that for auto parts."

"Then why do *you* think he put it here, Tom?"

"To hide it."

"Obviously," I said. "But why?"

"'Cause it's probably stolen."

"You think so?"

"'Course! Don't you?"

I laughed. "I'd like to think so. We ought to investigate."

"How?"

"I don't know yet. But if this *is* stolen stuff, there ought to be a way to figure out where it came from and whether the guy who used to live here stole it."

"Do you think he forgot about it? Isn't he worried your family will find it and think it's suspicious?"

I shrugged. How would I know? All I knew was that I couldn't sleep after that, daydreaming about cracking the case, arresting a thief, and being a hero.

The next morning Dad took my four friends and me to headquarters. The guys loved it, and it wasn't so bad being locked up for a minute when you had your friends with you. They plugged their ears while Dad demonstrated his marksmanship at the indoor range, and they all knew better than to even ask whether they could try shooting too.

We all peppered Dad with questions and said we'd love to be sheriff's deputies and help him out. He said we couldn't be trainees until we were eighteen and couldn't carry weapons until we were twenty-one.

"But what can we do now?" we kept asking.

Finally, just before it was time to go home, Dad took us into his office. He said he had an idea. "How would you boys like to be officially commissioned junior deputies?" he asked.

"Really? What would we do?"

"Just be alert and tell the police or the sheriff's department if you see anything suspicious."

Tom and I glanced at each other. "And by doing that, we would be deputies?"

Dad smiled. "You could call yourself the Kalamazoo County Junior Deputies."

"We finally have a name," Jonathan said. "'Course I still think The Five Stooges would have been better."

Dad told us that he traded souvenir shoulder patches with different police departments all over the world, and he showed us his collection. "Sometimes they also send along badges," he said. "But I don't collect those, and I've got about a dozen. If you promise never to use them to make people think you're something you're not, you can each have one. That'll make you an official junior deputy."

We all loved that idea.

"You mean we can't arrest people by flashing these?" Jonathan asked, holding his up to the light to see it glisten.

"That's exactly what I mean. These are real badges from cities in Florida, Ohio, Oklahoma, and California. They're just for fun—something to carry and play with."

"But they'll make us feel like real deputies."

"Good," Dad said. And he shook hands with each of us, welcoming us onto the squad and thanking us for our help in keeping the peace.

"Do you have one of those for Kate?" Tom asked.

"Sure," Dad said. "Does she want to be a junior deputy too?"

"We sort of promised her she could be part of our group."

Dad gave me a badge for Kate. She would be thrilled. The only problem was, I couldn't tell her about all of our cases. I didn't know if I could trust her to keep quiet about things until we were free to talk about them.

All the way home, Tom bugged my dad with questions about cases and criminals and how the police and sheriffs' offices caught people. He made up stories to see what Dad would say about catching whoever did the crime.

I could tell Dad was getting a little tired of all the questions, but he seemed as surprised as I was that Tom was talking so much. That just wasn't like Tom. Dad kept patiently answering, and just when I thought he was going to tell Tom he'd had enough, Tom asked one more.

"What if a guy stole some stuff and hid it somewhere and the police found out where he hid it?"

Dad said they would stake out the place, keep an eye on it, and arrest him when he came to get it.

"But what if he forgot where he'd put it and somebody found it and knew it was stolen?"

"It would be hard to connect to the thief unless he came to get it," Dad said.

"But what if you had an idea who did it? How would you get him to come for it?"

All of a sudden, Dad had warmed up. He was no longer tired of answering questions. He told a long story about a guy who stole some bicycles. The sheriff's office had no idea who had done it, but the bikes were all from a certain neighborhood.

"So we ran an ad in the newspaper, saying we were looking to buy a certain kind of bike—one of the very kind that had been stolen. Sure enough, someone answered the ad. A guy who'd lost his bike went with one of our undercover officers to see the bike that was for sale, and guess what? It was his own bike, with his name scratched under the seat and everything!"

Well, of course, that gave Tom and me an idea of how to remind the thief that he had left some stuff in the tunnels at our house. Later, I changed the subject with Dad and asked who we bought our house from.

"Actually," Dad said, "you'd be surprised. "The guy's name is Jack Shriber, and he makes his money running the county flea market—you know, where people bring their secondhand stuff and trade it or sell it cheap."

"He made enough money doing that to buy a big house like ours?"

"Well, he bought this house years ago when it was cheaper, but I understand he's moved into a very nice area and has even a bigger, more expensive home now."

"Dad, Tom and I have something we need to talk to you about."

The Setup

B y the time Tom and I finished telling my dad what we had discovered, Dad was looking pretty serious.

"How long were you going to wait before telling me about the tunnels?" Dad asked.

I shrugged. "I don't know. They seemed like a pretty cool secret. I didn't figure it would be long before Kate told you or Mom."

"You should have told me right away," Dad said.

"Why? Aren't we going to be allowed to play in there or to meet in the old coal bin?"

"I'm not saying that," Dad said. "But I'm going to have to check it out. I need to know how old those tunnels are, how well they are constructed, whether they're strong and safe. I also need to know there's a way out of there from both ends."

"There is," Tom said. "You'll see."

"But what if there's a collapse?" Dad said. "What if there's a fire or one end is locked?"

"I see what you mean," Tom said.

I was looking at the floor.

"You have to wonder if those tunnels were dug by Shriber, just to allow him to get to and from the garage with stolen merchandise," Dad said. "I'd be encouraged to know they're fairly modern. Then they probably would be stronger and hold up better. Let's take a look."

All five of us junior deputies went back down into the tunnels with Dad when we got home. Dad thought it would be better to leave Kate out of this adventure for the time being.

"She can help you on other cases if they aren't dangerous. We don't know about this one yet."

He had me give Kate her badge, though, and then Mom got her interested in something else while we explored.

The tunnels were just as dark and cold in the daytime as at night. Dad brought a gigantic light he used on patrol, and it lit up the whole area. When we got to the stored auto parts, he just stood there, his chin in his hand, looking and thinking.

Joel and Jon and Dan were amazed.

"You boys haven't touched any of this stuff yet, have you?"

"No."

"I need to make sure that what's in these boxes matches what it says on the outside, but I don't want to mess up any fingerprints if this is stolen stuff."

Dad put on gloves and used his pen to help open a few of the boxes. "These are top-of-the-line spark plugs, used for high performance racing cars," he said. "And most of these hub caps and wheel covers are for older, vintage sports cars, like Corvettes before 1970, MGs, cars like that."

"Are they stolen?"

"Hard to tell, but it sure looks like it. Shriber has plenty of storage areas, so he would keep these here only because he wanted them out of sight until he could sell them. I'd guess he'll come for them when there's demand. Of course, he *could* have just forgotten them. I'll check and see if we have any reports of stolen auto parts."

Dad then checked the structure of the tunnels. "These look like they were built right into the original foundation," he said. "Solid as rock. I guess it's OK for you to play in here, as long as you leave doors open on both ends."

While Dad was on the phone, the five of us guys met in the middle of the coal bin—to keep from brushing against the walls and getting dirty. We were so excited we hardly knew what to say. Here we were, just newly commissioned junior deputies, and we might already have a case. We wondered how much my dad might let us be involved.

He was on the phone quite a while. Finally he came back down and gathered us around him.

"Not only did I find out about the former owner of this house," he said, "I learned the history of this place and these tunnels. In the 1920s and 1930s, this house was actually used by gangsters associated with the mob in Chicago. They used to run bootleg whiskey out of here, transporting it through the tunnels to their cars. An old-timer in our office says his grandmother used to live next door, and she saw rivers of booze flowing down the street when federal agents raided the place years ago."

I could hardly believe we lived in a house that was once owned by mobsters.

"That's not all," Dad said. "The place was owned by another criminal before we bought it. I'll bet he'd be surprised to know he sold it to a deputy sheriff."

"So you found out this stuff was stolen by this Shriber guy?"

"We're pretty sure. You guys found this case and brought it to me, so I'm going to let you have a little part in it. Our records show that the Kalamazoo Police Department arrested a couple of Jack Shriber's part-time employees more than a year ago. They were selling auto parts, just like the ones hidden in the tunnel, and we traced them to the burglary at the Hot Rods, Etc. store in Portage. They both went to jail, but we never recovered the rest of the merchandise, and they never mentioned Shriber's name.

"But the stuff stored in here proves he was behind it and that they were stealing for him. He's been in trouble before for trafficking in stolen merchandise, but he's never gone to jail for it. Nobody could prove he stole anything or hired someone to steal it, so all they could get him on was possession of stolen property. These days it's hard to send anybody to jail for something like that."

"But he had to have something to do with this stuff," Jonathan suggested. "Otherwise, what's it doing under his old house?"

"Right," Dad said. "Now we have to get him to come back for it. Then we've got him."

"How are you going to do that?" I asked.

"I have a plan," Dad said. "And I could use your help."

We looked at each other, smiling.

"Now, obviously I can't involve any of you in actually catching the guy. That would be too dangerous. But I can use you in tricking him into coming here, and then we can figure out a way to trap him in the tunnel until my officers can move in and take him."

"Cool!"

I think Dad could tell we were a little too eager, so he calmed us down and told us how important this all was. We tried to assure him that we knew, and we tried to look more serious. It wasn't easy.

"If you guys can follow directions and do everything I say, you can help me with this today."

"Today?"

"This afternoon. Want to go to the flea market and see if you can trick Shriber into coming over here to steal the stuff he already stole?"

"Sure!"

"All right then. Gather around and listen. I'll tell you what I need done, and you can decide who's going to do what."

Dad mapped out a great master plan. We were to ride our bikes to the old drive-in theater next to the county fairgrounds where Shriber held his huge flea market every Saturday and Sunday afternoon.

We were supposed to mosey around through all the exhibits of cheap junk, and then start asking questions at Shriber's own booth. If it all went right, we'd wind up getting to talk to the man himself and lure him into Dad's web.

It took almost a half hour for Dad to explain what had to happen at the flea market, then we met by ourselves to give out assignments. It was almost like a play. Everybody had a part, something to say. We were so nervous we all started laughing, but then Tom or I would grow serious and remind the guys that we had to do this right or we'd make Shriber suspicious.

We went and found Dad again and told him we thought we were ready.

He pretended to be Shriber and made us walk through the whole plan, everything we were going to say and all that. "I'm impressed," he said, smiling. "You guys are really good. Remember, this is a sting operation."

"What's that?" Jonathan asked.

"We're setting the guy up so he buys into our little trap. Then we sting him. And the most important thing about a sting is what?"

"To make him think it's his idea," Tom said.

Everyone looked surprised, even Dad.

"How did you know that?" Dad asked.

"I used to do a lot of hustling," Tom said. "You make a guy think you've got something he might want, then you pull it away at the last minute and make him almost come begging for it. That makes it his idea, and he never suspects you're going to swindle him."

"Exactly," Dad said. "So when you get Shriber interested, when he thinks you might want what he has to offer, you want to act very skeptical and uninterested all of a sudden. Make him sell *you* on the idea."

Dad said he would take Mom and Kate to the flea market too, just so he could keep an eye on us. "Don't let anyone know you even know me," he said, "because lots of people know who I am. Just know that we'll be around there somewhere. Everybody know his part?"

We all nodded, and if the rest of the guys were like me, they were silently praying and repeating their parts over and over. We had to do it right, and it had to be convincing.

After lunch Mom and Dad and Kate drove to the flea market. The five junior deputies rode our bikes and got there probably a half hour later.

I had never been to the flea market before, but Dan and Joel had. The rest of us were surprised at how much cool stuff was there. We got so interested in looking at all the junk at such low prices, we almost forgot why we were there.

Finally, it was time to make our move. We moseyed around until we wound up at Jack Shriber's booth. Jack was nowhere to be seen, but that was no surprise since he owned the whole flea market and was probably busy with other things.

His wife, Eunice, was a big woman with a name tag on her blouse. She was loud and friendly and seemed to try to help everyone at once. She came past Dan and Tom and me and asked us if we needed anything.

"No, thanks," Tom said. "We're just looking."

"Well, don't touch anything," she said, smiling. "You break it, you buy it. You steal it, and you answer to Jack."

"Yes, ma'am."

We watched as she came up to Joel and Jon with the same message. They were looking at brand new parts for Corvettes. They played their parts perfectly.

"We won't touch them," Joel said. "We just want to see 'em."

"My friend's cousin has a Corvette," Jon said, his red hair bright in the sun. "Wonder if he needs any hub caps."

"These aren't hub caps, honey," Eunice Shriber said. "These here are wheel covers."

"What's the difference?" Jon said.

"Well, if you don't know the difference, you're probably not interested."

"We're not, but our friend's cousin might be."

"What year is his Corvette? These are new, for the late models."

Both boys shrugged.

"Well, when you know a little more about whether he's lookin' and what he might be lookin' for, you let me know."

"He's here," Joel said. "We'll tell him to come and look."

"You do that," she said. "Now, excuse me." And she moved to another shopper.

Joel turned and smiled at us, and Jonathan gave us the thumbs-up sign. We pretended not to notice.

We all kept walking, checking out the cheap watches and toys and used clothes. About half an hour later, Dan and Tom and I got back around to the Shriber booth.

We went to the same display of wheel covers that Jon and Joel had looked at, and pretty soon Eunice came over. Before she could give us the usual lecture, Big Dan started with his part. "These can't be real," he said.

"Oh, yes, they are," Eunice said.

"They have to be imitations, and they'll probably peel and change colors," Daniel said.

"No," Eunice insisted, "they're the genuine article. And they're half what you'd pay for them at a Chevy dealer."

93

"Well, why would somebody pay that much for a car and then want cheap wheel covers?"

"Just to save money," she said.

"Are these genuine? Made by General Motors?"

"Well, no. We get them from another supplier. But they're every bit as good, and because we buy so many, we get them at a better price and can offer 'em at half price. You boys don't get your fingers all over 'em now, you hear?"

We nodded.

"Toby," Tom said, "doesn't your cousin have Corvettes?"

I nodded, pretending not to be interested.

"Corvettes plural?" Mrs. Shriber repeated.

I didn't say anything.

"Yeah!" Tom said. "He's got four or five! He collects 'em."

"Three," I said. "He's only got three."

"Well, does he need anything for them?" Eunice said. "We have lots of parts for that kind of a car."

I shrugged. "I don't know. Probably. He can't use these though."

"Why not? He already have wheel covers?"

"No. In fact, I think he's lookin' for wheel covers for all three of his cars. But they're old. He keeps 'em looking like they did when they were made in the sixties."

"In the sixties!" she repeated. "He's got three Corvettes from the sixties?"

I nodded and began to walk away.

"Wait a minute, son," she said. "Does your cousin live around here?"

I nodded, still not looking at her.

"I might be able to come up with some 1960s-style wheel covers for Corvettes."

I shrugged again. "He'd need twelve. I'd be surprised if you could get twelve."

"I just might."

I shook my head and turned away.

Tom hung back, and Mrs. Shriber said, "Tell him I'll talk to my husband and see what we can do."

"I don't know anything about it," Tom said.

"Just tell him," she said. "Come back in a little while, and I'll have Jack here."

It was working.

The Sting

A little while later, when we drifted back past Jack Shriber's booth, I could see out of the corner of my eye that Jack's wife was pointing me out to him.

"Say!" Jack said, coming over. "Which of you was looking for wheel covers for sixties Corvettes?"

Dan and Tom pointed to me, but I didn't say anything.

"Well?" Jack said. "Are you?"

"Not me," I said.

"I heard that you were."

"Well, it's my cousin, and he would probably want a dozen for his three cars, but he wouldn't want new stuff. He'd want original stuff."

"What if I told you I had both?"

"Both what? How could it be new and original? You mean nobody's used this stuff for more than thirty years?"

"That's what I'm tellin' you. I have a source. He bought up lots of stuff like that and has been sitting on it for years. It's expensive, but it's the real thing."

"I don't think so," I said. "If it's that good, it has to be hot."

"Hot!" Jack said. "You'll never catch me dealing in stolen merchandise!"

"Then where is it?" I asked.

"Well, it's not the type of thing I'd sell at a flea market," Jack said. "If your cousin really wants it, he'll have to come to me."

I shrugged. "I don't have any idea if he wants it." I began to walk away again. I was so good at this stuff that even I was amazed.

Jack followed me, holding out his business card. "Tell him to call me! He'll never find stuff this good anywhere else."

"Then how did *you* find it?" Tom asked.

"I told you. I have a source."

We walked away, with Jack calling after us, "Have him call!"

The five of us regrouped in the parking lot, and after making sure no one could see us, we met with my dad and told him everything.

He told us what to do.

About an hour later Tom and Dan and I went to see Jack Shriber.

"You gonna call that cousin?" he asked.

"Already did," I said. "He doesn't believe it."

"That's his loss," Jack said.

"He doesn't trust you," I said.

"What's not to trust? Did you tell him who I am? Did you tell him I own this place? I'm as trustworthy as he's gonna find!"

"He said if you were serious you could have the stuff for him to see right here tomorrow afternoon."

"I can't do that!" Shriber said. "I told you. This prime merchandise is not something you bring to a flea market."

"I don't care one way or the other," I said. "That's what he told me, that's all."

Shriber was turning colors. "All right," he said. "You bring him back here, tomorrow afternoon late, like four or so. I'll have a selection for him."

"No promises," I said.

"Hey, I'm doin' what he said. I'm bringin' the stuff!"

"I'll tell him, but I can't make him do anything he doesn't want to do."

"You just tell him! I'll be here with a good deal."

One more time we walked away as if we didn't care what happened.

Dad said we had really baited the hook. "Unless Jack Shriber has more of that stuff hidden somewhere else, I expect him to try to come and get it. He may even give me a call."

"Why would he do that?" Tom said. "Wouldn't that give him away?"

"I don't know how he's going to get to the stuff otherwise," Dad said. "We'll just have to wait and see."

Needless to say, my mom was pretty upset with the whole deal. She said Dad was exposing my friends and me to unnecessary risks.

"I know about this guy, hon," Dad said. "He's dishonest, but he's not dangerous. Anyway, the boys won't even have to see him again."

"Then how is Toby supposed to go back and see him tomorrow afternoon with this made-up cousin?"

"He won't go back," Dad said. "If Jack doesn't call or come here, we just drop it. He won't ever know what happened. If he comes here, we'll catch him with the stuff."

The phone rang.

Mom answered it and turned white. "Just a moment," she said and covered the mouthpiece. "Philip, it's for you. It's Jack Shriber."

Dad raised his eyebrows and held a finger to his lips.

We were all quiet and listened to his end of the conversation.

"Hey, Jack, how are ya? . . . Great . . . Oh, we love it. You kept the place up nice, and we're settling in real well. Just perfect. What can I do for you? . . . In the garage? . . . Um, yeah, OK. Well, listen, we'll be at church tomorrow morning—we leave here about eight-thirty, and we get back about one. You think it would take longer than that? . . . If it does, we can just park outside for a while. No problem . . . Yeah, I'll leave the garage door unlocked. If you wouldn't mind locking it if you leave before we get back, I'd appreciate it . . . You're welcome."

Dad hung up, and we slapped hands all around.

"What was that all about?" Big Dan said.

"He bit big time," Dad said. "He asked if I still had the pulley in the rafters in the garage—the one he used to raise the engines out of his cars to work on them. I told him it was still there, and he asked if he could sneak his van in there sometime to work on it. Said it wouldn't take long. You know how the rest of the conversation went."

"What's he gonna do?" Tom asked. "Go into the tunnel through the garage and take the stuff out?"

"Looks like it. Just the way he did when he lived here."

"Do the junior deputies get to jump him?" Jonathan asked, laughing.

"Not on your life," Dad said. "I'll have officers ready to move in. You can help me get the area ready though. And somebody is going to have to lock him out of the garage once he gets into the tunnel."

"You're going to lock him in the tunnel?"

Dad nodded. "I want to force him to try to crawl out through the coal feeder. That's where we'll be waiting for him."

"Are you telling me these boys are not going to church and Sunday school tomorrow morning?" Mom asked.

"If my guess is right," Dad said, "we'll just be a little late. We'll leave in both cars at the usual time, just in case someone is watching. You take Kate to church. I'll double back and park out of sight in the alley, and I'll get the across-the-street neighbors to let us park a couple of squad cars in their garages."

"How are we going to lock Shriber in the tunnel?"

"His van will be a couple of feet from the workbench that blocks the door," Dad said. "We need someone who's small enough to crawl in there but strong enough to push that bench back in front of the door. Then that same person will have to wedge something between the van and the bench. No way that tunnel door will budge when he tries to come back out."

"And you're going to block the door from the tunnel to the coal bin too?"

"We could, but I want him to be able to get to the little coal-feeder door. That will be the best place to grab him, while he's jammed in there."

"But how do you keep him from getting out of the coal bin and into the basement?"

"We'll nail that door shut. He'll have only one choice, and it'll be the wrong one. He'll have to shove his merchandise out the trapdoor first, then shove his dolly out—or whatever he uses to move the stuff—and then he'll have to get out himself. He's going to be mighty surprised to see Lake County sheriff's deputies when he comes out."

"I can't wait!" Jonathan said.

"I want to be here!" Kate said.

"Don't even dream about it," Mom said.

Mom wanted to talk with me in private. We went to my room.

"You know why this scares me, don't you, Toby?"

I nodded.

"Tell me why, so I know that you know."

"Because you already lost one son, and you don't want to lose another."

She bit her lip.

I didn't mean to be so blunt, but I didn't know how else to say it.

"That's right," she said finally, whispering.

"You're not going to lose me, Mom. Dad wouldn't get me into anything really dangerous, and God will protect me. You've always told me that."

"I know," she said. "You don't hold it against God that He took Jason, do you?"

"God took him? I thought you said God allowed him to die but that God isn't the one who causes people to die."

"Well, yes," she said. "Satan is the author of death. But we prayed that God would heal Jason, remember?"

"It's what I prayed for every day."

"Does it bother you that God didn't answer our prayers?"

Somehow I knew Mom was asking herself the same questions she was asking me.

"Mom, you and Dad said that God *always* answers—just not always the way we want. I don't understand why Jason had to die, but I'm trying to trust God the same way you are."

Mom couldn't speak. Her chin was quivering. She stood and hugged me. "You're being a good example to me," she said.

"I just believe what you tell me, Mom. I may not always act like it, but I don't know what else to do. I trust you, and I trust Dad."

"And we're trying to trust God, even when it's hard," she said. "You just keep doing that, and we'll survive this thing."

"I don't mean to change the subject, Mom," I said, "but does this mean you're going to trust Dad and let me do this?"

She actually laughed. Mom hadn't done that very much lately. "I will trust your father too, yes," she said.

None of us slept much that night. Dad walked us through the plan and had us nail the coal bin door shut from the basement side. We made a huge mess of it, but there was no way anyone would be able to come through that door from the other side.

In the garage he found an old pallet and some blankets that would make it thicker if it needed to be.

"How are you going to decide who should push the workbench back and wedge something between it and the van?" Dad asked. "I doubt Joel or Jonathan could move the bench. That leaves three of you."

"I'd be the hardest to see," Big Dan said. "But I don't know if I could fit between the van and the bench."

That left Tom and me. Each of us tried moving the bench by himself. No good. It would take both of us. We set up a spot to hide in the garage. Dad set it up with his men to be waiting in the garages across the street early in the morning.

We all dressed for church and took off in our two cars just before eight-thirty. Mom gave Dad a worried look, but I could tell they had already discussed it and that she approved. She trusted him and said she would be praying for us.

A couple of blocks away, Dad circled around and came back through an alley. He left the car hidden.

Joel, Jon, and Dan went in the house and waited in Mom's sewing room on the second floor, which gave them a view of the garage and the side of the house where Shriber would have to crawl out. Dad made sure Tom and I were hidden in a corner of the garage behind an old desk and a refrigerator, then he hurried across the street to wait with the other deputies.

At about nine o'clock a van pulled into the driveway. Jack Shriber opened the garage door, backed the van in, and shut it off. He closed the door and immediately dragged the workbench away from the tunnel entrance. He opened the door, then hauled a dolly out of the back of the van and shoved it into the tunnel ahead of him.

Dad had told us to wait until we were sure he was far enough into the tunnels to not hear us. Then we scrambled over and quietly shut the door, pushed the bench back into position, and wedged the wood pallet between the van and the bench. It fit almost perfectly.

Tom and I ran out the side door of the garage and waved, which was the signal for Dad and his guys to move into position.

The garage doors on the other side of the street opened, and two squad cars came barreling out. One parked right in front of our garage door where Shriber's van was. The other parked on the street just out of sight of the coal-feeder door. One deputy waited by the garage door, gun drawn, just in case Shriber somehow broke out into the garage. The others waited with my dad near the coal-feeder door but not where Shriber could see them.

Tom and I climbed a tree behind the garage, where we had a perfect view. We waved and smiled at the other junior deputies in the window of Mom's sewing room on the second floor.

In a few minutes we heard banging and pounding in the garage. It went on for over a minute. We wondered what kind of damage Jack was doing to his vehicle, pushing the door into the bench into the pallet and into the van.

He finally gave up. A minute later we heard banging from inside the coal bin. He was trying to get out through the basement. He had no better luck there. Now all eyes were on that little metal door at ground level.

Soon it opened inward, and Jack propped it somehow. Then box after box of auto parts was shoved out. Then a dozen wheel covers. Finally, just as Dad had predicted, here came the dolly. Next came a big flashlight. Then we saw dirty hands at the bottom of the opening. Then Jack's red face. He was squinting against the light.

He pulled himself into position and tried to wriggle through the narrow opening. It was all Tom and I could do to keep from laughing out loud and pointing at him—filthy, sweating, struggling, panting, inching his way out. Finally he got his hands on the ground and pulled himself along, crawling the last yard until his feet flopped free.

Jack Shriber lay there for a second catching his breath, and when he sat up and started to stand, he saw five uniformed Kalamazoo County deputy sheriffs in a half circle around him. He slumped to the ground, caught red-handed.

What he didn't know, of course, was that he had been done in by the Kalamazoo County Junior Deputies, whose pictures would be on the front page of the *Kalamazoo Gazette* the next day.

We were heroes, and we were open for business.